Sean,
Thanks for swooping
A Copy. And Thanks for
Being A Cool dude & A Great
Friend.

-Will

Animal Speak

The Book of Teachings

By W. F. Mick

Strategic Book Publishing and Rights Co.

Copyright © 2012.
All rights reserved by W. F. Mick.

Book Design/Layout by Kalpart. Visit www.kalpart.com

No part of this book may be reproduced or transmitted in any form or by any means, graphic, electronic, or mechanical including photocopying, recording, taping or by any information retrieval system, without the permission in writing of the publisher.

Strategic Book Publishing and Rights Co.
12620 FM 1960, Suite A4-507
Houston TX 77065
www.spbra.com

ISBN: 978-1-62212-134-2

Gail ...

You have been like a mother to me — through everything

Thank You

Love,
W. F.

Table of Contents

Chapter One — Animal Speak 7

Chapter Two — Man and Dog 14

Chapter Three — The Departure 29

Chapter Four — Elliot 36

Chapter Five — Weather and Woods 42

Chapter Six — Lumen 49

Chapter Seven — The Oxen Fields 55

Chapter Eight — The Speakers Village 62

Chapter Nine — The Book of Teachings 73

Chapter Ten — Gloomy Tidings 86

Chapter Eleven — Blackfoot Quarry 97

Chapter Twelve — The Return of the Liar 102

Chapter Thirteen — The One in Charge 110

Chapter Fourteen — The Battle of Blackfoot 113

Chapter One: Animal Speak

Far across the most dangerous seas and beyond, lies the mystical world of Varia. Deep in this land, past the deserts and mountains, the forests and the seas, lies the gentle valley of Oakhill. Tucked far from the prying eyes of travelers or passersby, shrouded in the shadow of the beautiful mountains surrounding them, everything in Oakhill ran smoothly, like flowing water from the most dazzling stream. Oakhill is a place of peace, prosperity, and love, and it's here where the story begins.

Lila Lavender was planting tomatoes in her garden when the rain let loose on the villagers, drenching them all in icy-cold, walnut-sized droplets. Lila ran from her garden to her hut and hastily started a fire.

Every member in the village had a particular duty to perform daily in order for the village to survive. There was the handful of fisherman who caught fish by the lake near the mountains. The gardeners and livestock keepers kept a fresh supply of fruits, veggies, and eggs for the village meals. The hunters patrolled the woods for deer and rabbit, and the shaman provided the medical assistance and valuable life skills and advice for the villagers. Every night, the village would eat a spectacular meal together at the massive table in the town square. When the feast was done, they would gather by the fireside and tell tales and stories of the most magnificent kinds.

The most famous tale, and by far the most exciting, was the tale of the mighty people who had been given the gift of Animal Speak. The story tells of the people who traveled across the sea from Elda to Varia, seeking out those like them and teaching them the ways of the Speakers. They lived their lives according to the earth, traveling far and wide with their animal companions, seeking out treasures beyond all descriptions, but most of all, they defended and protected the less fortunate from the growing dangers of man's cruelty and greed. There had never before been a Speaker in Oakhill and the villagers had never come across one, having never ventured past the mountains into the lands beyond. The tale was told mostly for the entertainment of the children, and most of the villagers, with the exception of the elders, regarded the whole thing as a fairy tale, and paid no heed to it.

The storm raged on, pounding the villagers' little huts with rain and wind. Lila was now tending the fire she had started in her own hut, its crackling orange embers and flames sending warmth to every corner, heating her cold, rain-soaked body. As she cut up potatoes and mushrooms for her stew, something moving outside caught her attention. Peering out of her window into the rain and wind, just before the wood line, she saw it. There was something massive moving through the trees. Was it a deer or perhaps something worse? As she focused harder, peering at the trees with extreme difficulty, she saw that it was a dog.

The dog was massive; even from far off, she could tell that. Lila was sure it would have reached her waist if she were to stand next to it. It had a reddish gold coat, speckled with beautiful white spots. It had a strong look to it, as if it could take down a full-grown warrior with ease. It was sitting next to a rather large oak tree, and unless Lila was much mistaken — and she hoped she was — the dog seemed to be looking directly at her.

Nothing made a sound as the two stared at each other for a few minutes; even the rain seemed to have muted itself, though it did not dampen its flow. As Lila began to wonder when the dog would move, there was a blinding flash of lightning and a mighty *boom* of thunder from above, and the dog had vanished. Lila blinked. Thinking she must have missed it departing in the flash, she returned to her soup and turned away from the window, putting the dog out of her mind.

A week passed since Lila spotted the dog, and she completely forgot about it. The rain, however, didn't vanish as quickly as the dog had. Throughout the week, the villagers' moods had drastically worsened as the storm raged on. The rain had flooded the lake, which made everything a very unpleasant, muddy mess. Lila was wandering by the lake, looking for stray lily pads for the evening soup, in hopes of having something hot in her belly to cheer her up a bit, when the dog appeared once more. As the wind whipped her soaking wet hair into her face, she saw the dog trotting along at a quick pace, coming from the northern side of the lake, its thick paws thudding and splashing through the mud. Once again, and most strangely, it was staring fixedly at her.

It was coming closer now; Lila believed the dog was after her bread in the basket by her feet. She reached down for the basket just as the dog broke into a heavy run. But she was too late; the dog was upon her. It bowled her right over, knocking her off her feet and sending her splashing into the flooded, muddy water. As she raised herself to her feet, spluttering and wiping mud from her face, she spotted the dog, a basket in its mouth, disappearing into the black woods in the distance. Lila trudged home cursing, covered in smelly mud, soaked to the bone, hungry and altogether miserable.

The next morning, Lila decided to pay a visit to Prentice, the villagers' shaman, hoping to get some insight on her peculiar animal visitor. Prentice had witnessed a good deal in his time, and he was the only citizen of Oakhill who had seen the lands beyond. As a matter of fact, he came from a dreadful land away in the south, where men were wicked and cruel. Escaping these lands, Prentice came upon the valley when lost in the mountains. Finding it very comfy and peaceful, he decided to stay there. Over time, the villagers grew to love him, as he helped them to cope with their lives and taught them the ways of medicine and earth. Prentice's life was a very sad tale to tell, though no one in Oakhill knew about his mysterious past, and they refrained from questioning him about it. It is very disrespectful to pry into another person's privacy, and manners and courtesy go a very long way in Varia, even when facing your mortal enemy.

Lila approached the shaman's hut, which was the largest but just as roughly built as all the others. Prentice did not believe in elegance or fancy demeanors. He was a man of the earth and people; he was pure. She knocked on his heavy wooden door. There was a cough and a scuffling, and the door creaked open slowly. Smoke billowed out in spirals as the fresh crisp air from the storm rushed in. A moment later, Prentice appeared in the doorway, smiling down at her.

"Lila," he said softly. "To what do I owe this wonderful yet unexpected surprise?"

Lila sighed slightly, returning the smile he had given her, looking into his wise blue eyes.

"I need some advice and I don't know who else to ask, really," she pleaded to him, somewhat embarrassed at the tears now running down her face. "I don't know what it wants or if it's even real. But I'm very worried."

Prentice smiled and gestured for her to enter the hut. Prentice's hut was calm and cozy. The fire was warm and inviting, and the incense stick burning on the mantle smelled of sweet honeysuckles. The overall effect of the hut seemed to wipe all stress and anxiety clean away from you.

"Come sit and calm down, my dear," he said, chuckling slightly and pulling a chair from the table and leading her to it. "You mustn't let this dull weather get to you, too. Please tell me what is troubling you, my dear."

"I have a strange animal that won't leave me alone," she said, sniffing slightly. "I know I must sound so silly right now."

"Not at all," said Prentice, his voice full of wonder and interest now. "Please, go on."

So Lila recounted the bizarre story of the dog's appearance and disappearance, and how it seemed to only have eyes for her. When she had finished her tale, Prentice simply gazed at her curiously over the table. Lila wondered if he was wondering if she was losing her mind.

"I'm not going mad, am I?" she asked him fearfully.

"Mad?" said Prentice, looking confused slightly. "No, no. you are most certainly not going mad, dear," he finished wisely.

"But how do you know for certain?" she asked desperately.

"I don't," he said quietly. "I do know that animals have a very strange and peculiar way of telling a person something. They make the person figure out the bulk of it and are there to mostly guide you along, to show you the right way, so to speak."

"I see," said Lila in wonder.

"You should follow it," said Prentice from across the table.

Lila gaped at him, utterly perplexed.

"Why on earth would I want to do that?" she said, sounding as if she now thought that Prentice might be going mad himself.

Prentice smiled and took a long pull on a beautifully hand-carved wooden pipe and watched the smoke exit through the window before answering.

"I assure you, Lila, I'm not going mad," he said smiling, a twinkle in his eye. "As for the dog, well like I said before, follow it. This animal seems to have chosen you of all the villagers here. Don't be hasty to rid yourself of it. It may need your help."

Lila sighed deeply. Everything seemed to make sense to her now. She would follow the dog if it reappeared again, and this time she would not lose it.

"Thank you, Prentice," she said graciously to the old man.

Prentice rose to his feet, gesturing Lila to do the same.

"You are most welcome, my dear," he said warmly to her.

Lila left the hut, feeling much more relaxed than when she had entered it. Even the rain couldn't dampen her spirits.

* * *

As the week dragged on in Oakhill, so did the rain. The atmosphere all around was dull and glum. Many of the villagers had retreated permanently to their huts, even at mealtimes. The hunters stayed indoors as well, leaving the food gathering up to the gardeners and fisherman, which thoroughly annoyed most of the villagers.

"They are lazy and no good," some would say.

"Drat 'em," others would say.

Lila continued to keep her eyes peeled for the dog over the next few days, but saw neither hide nor hair of it. It was nearly two weeks after her talk with Prentice until she saw the dog again. She was walking from the lake toward her hut when she spotted it. It was sitting stock still in her garden, staring directly at her. The dog barked loudly and darted off in the direction of the forest. Lila wasn't going to miss her chance again. Running into her hut as fast as she could, she grabbed a heavy cloak, threw it over her shoulders, and darted out the door in pursuit of the dog.

The dog was sitting by a large tree on the wood line, waiting for her quietly. As she drew nearer, the dog turned and trotted ahead of her, stopping occasionally to watch her stumble and struggle through the wet bramble, brush, and overgrowth. The rain pounded on them heavier and heavier as each minute passed. Lila struggled on, trying desperately to keep her eyes on the dog and to keep up with its now quickened pace. Water was running down her face into her eyes from the relentless storm. They trekked on and on, as the threat of nightfall crept up on them slowly but surely from all areas.

Finally, the trees became less thick, but this meant the rain soaked them more as they walked through gaps in the trees. Then quite suddenly, with no warning, the trees cleared completely, revealing a spectacular view of the black and ominous mountains that surrounded the valley of Oakhill. They had reached the very outskirts of the valley itself.

The sky was dark now. Night had fallen but the rain pounded on, the peaks of the mountains hidden from view by black clouds. All that could be heard was rain, wind, and the rushing of water issuing from a stream that was running out the mouth of a cave at the foot of the closest mountain. Then a shrill cry rang out, sending icy shivers down Lila's spine. The dog gave a mighty howl next to her. The cry rang out once more, and Lila realized it was coming from the cave ahead of her. She looked down at the dog, which had begun to whine, staring at the cave's entrance.

"Is it safe?" she asked the dog, at the same time feeling silly for talking to it.

The dog gave a bark and pushed Lila toward the cave with its rather large nose.

"Okay, okay," she said to it, "I'll go in."

The dog barked once more, and then lay upon the ground, staring at the cave. Lila stood up straight and marched toward the cave, her body shaking and shivering with cold and fear, just as another cry rang out, echoing madly on the cave's walls. The cry rang out again, and Lila realized that it was the cry of a child. There was a baby in this cave! She took a deep breath and entered the cave.

She made her way through the cave, her feet submerged in the icy stream flowing out toward the woods and her village and lake. The cries were growing more distinct now as she stumbled blindly on, her hands using the slimy cave wall as direction. She could hear a faint dripping ahead of her, and as each drop fell into whatever was ahead, she felt it was vibrating all through her bones.

Splash!

Suddenly and without warning, Lila had fallen into an icy pool of water. Standing up and spluttering, she regained her wits and looked around. She heard a slight stir to her left and looked down. There it was, wrapped in a dirty bundle of blankets and rags — a baby boy. Lila stooped down and picked up the child and cradled it in her arms, where it seemed very content, sucking on its thumb. Around the boy's wrist was a bracelet of pure silver, with letters etched on its top.

It read simply: Stanley.

With a dreadful pang in her heart, she saw what had been lying next to the child. A beautiful, brown-haired woman was lying on the ground, her eyes closed. Lila leaned down and felt the woman's wrist — ice cold. She had been dead for maybe three days now. After a few moments, Lila turned away with little Stanley in her arms and made her way back out of the cave, following the rushing water. When she reached the opening, she met the dog, which was wagging its tail furiously at the sight of them.

"It's all right, dear," she said gently to the dog. "He's quite in good health, just a little cold and hungry."

The dog barked loudly and darted off toward the mountains, leaving Lila and Stanley completely alone. Lila looked down at the baby, now sleeping quietly in her arms.

"You are indeed a miracle of the earth, my dear," she said softly, smiling at him gently. "Now let's get you home, Stanley."

And at that very moment, the rain stopped and the storm passed, revealing the moon shining brightly against the billions of stars. Lila smiled at them as she made her way home with Stanley. As for the dog, it would not be seen by anyone for many long years.

Chapter Two: Man and Dog

A man in a tattered red cloak was stalking a deer that was wondering through the brush of the forest. His hood hid his brown eyes and wiry hair from view, revealing only a strong chin, and hard, lined cheekbones. He was gripping a long staff made of ash, and he was moving so swiftly and quietly a mouse wouldn't have turned a whisker toward him, even if he had trodden right next to it. He stooped down to examine some deer tracks, grabbing the leaves and twigs strewn about the ground and crushing them in his hand. He then gave them a hearty sniff. From this, the man deduced that the deer was making its way north. He had to be quick now; he had to pick up his pace considerably. If he didn't catch the deer within the next hour, he would have to return to the village, once again empty-handed. Not that any of them would be surprised. They probably expected it, he thought glumly to himself.

The man was not a hunter, but a shaman of the earth, a man of wisdom and healing, not a killer of animals. He was rather fond of them quite honestly, preferring to watch and study them, rather than finding out what they taste like when you slaughter them. The village hunters, however, were at the mercy of a sickness that only Prentice, his mentor, could heal. The healing process took a few days, however, and it was closing down on day three of having to do the hunters' work, as well as his own. He hoped they would be back on their feet tomorrow, though, as he was growing weary and exhausted of coming home with nothing, only to receive dark, murderer's looks from the very hungry villagers. At least he was trying, he thought miserably to himself, though it did nothing to improve his mood.

He picked up his pace to a light jog and headed north, going as silently as he could manage in the thick brush and bramble that cluttered the forest floor. He had never been this deep into the forest before; the path was now unfamiliar and nearly impossible to navigate through, due to the uncontrollable undergrowth and thickets growing sporadically all over. All along, though, the man trudged on, a strong sense of determination about him. The rushing of a stream met his ears and he slowed his pace, knowing that the beast would probably stop to take a drink before continuing on its way.

He spotted the deer a slight way ahead of him, drinking from the cool, crisp stream. Holding his staff firmly in his hands, his heart thudding through his chest, he made his way forward, using all of his might and concentration to stay silent and not make any sudden sound that would potentially spook the deer. Suddenly, there was a mighty scuffling from somewhere to his right, making the deer look up, its ears pricked for a sign of danger, listening intently. The man had to act now, or the deer would surely escape. Before he could even make a move, however, or even lift his staff, a massive dog, the largest he had ever seen, leaped from the thicket and bounded upon the deer.

The dog was a reddish gold in color, with white spots speckled and splashed on its powerful body. It had strong muscles, and an immensely powerful jaw. Within an instant, the dog had brought the deer to the ground, dead. It turned its head and looked at the man, wagging its tail silently. The man hesitated; he did not know this dog, nor had he ever seen it before, but he had this odd feeling that the dog knew him. It stared placidly at him, its tail continuing to wag. Finally, the man acted. He walked right over to the dog, stooped down and picked up the dead deer and slung it over his shoulders. He then looked down at the dog.

"Thank you," he said to it rather awkwardly.

He then began to turn away to head in the direction of the path leading to the village, when it happened.

"No problem," said the dog casually, and turned off and ran into the forest's depths, disappearing from view.

The man nearly dropped the deer.

The man returned home a short while later, with the deer slung over his shoulders and a broad grin on his face. The villagers nearest to the wood line bounded out of their huts, cheering and clapping for joy as the man made his way through the village with his catch. The man laid the deer upon the massive, iron woodstove that was used for cooking the meals, which was already heavily laden with various mushrooms, potatoes, fruits, sprouts, and wild onions. The man spotted his caretaker making her way toward him through the cheering crowd, beaming broadly.

Lila approached the man and hugged him in her arms. It had been many long years since she had emerged from the cave with little Stanley in her arms. Her hair was now wispy, no longer auburn, but a silky white. Her reactions were much slower now, but her caring nature and the warming effect of her smile had grown tremendously over the years. She smiled at Stanley, who grinned back broadly at her.

"I brought dinner," he said happily, gesturing toward the deer.

"You look exhausted," Lila said, looking him up and down.

"You don't know the half of it," said Stanley wearily.

"You must tell me," said a voice from behind them, as a hand clapped on Stanley's shoulder. "How did you manage to bag that deer, Stanley?"

It was Prentice, his mentor, his teacher, and by far one of the wisest and most insightful men he knew. Prentice himself had aged a great deal as well, though his reactions and his senses remained as honed as ever and better than most young men in the village.

"I was under the impression that I schooled a shaman, not a hunter," he said sternly, but his face was fighting back a smile.

"Don't think too highly of me just yet," said Stanley, smiling at his teacher. "I had help."

"Help?" repeated Prentice and Lila simultaneously.

"Yes, help," said Stanley again.

"Help from whom?" asked Prentice curiously.

"Just an animal — a dog — what's the big deal?" Stanley said, somewhat offhanded.

He wasn't sure why they both looked amazed and curious at this. He didn't think anything of it, so why were they now looking at him with a sort of new wonder in their eyes?

"Was this a large dog," Prentice asked him, "a golden red in color, with heavy white spots?"

Stanley exclaimed, completely amazed this time.

"Because we have seen it before," said Lila, answering him.

Prentice examined his pupil for a moment, considering him slightly.

"After tonight's feast, come to my hut," he said seriously. "We must talk, but not here. There are too many prying eyes about. I will explain everything, but I must be cautious here. I say no more. I'll see you tonight."

And without another word, he turned on his heel and darted off in the direction of his hut, leaving Stanley altogether bemused and speechless. He turned to Lila, who he noticed was looking rather shifty and anxious.

"Would you mind explaining all of this?" he asked her, slightly annoyed.

"No," said Lila firm and stern.

"No?" Stanley asked her, his confusion mounting.

"Yes, no," she said softly. "It's not for me to tell you, but for you to discover yourself, my dear.

Stanley stood rooted to the spot for a few minutes, wondering how he should feel. This was all very perplexing, not to mention frustrating. He sighed to himself and walked back to his hut, hoping that tonight, his questions would be answered and his problem solved.

That night, the entire village gathered for a splendid feast of venison. Stanley was treated like a hero that night by the villagers. Even the hunters, who did not get along with him much, came and congratulated him on catching such a fine deer on his own. After the wonderful dinner that made him feel like his trousers were at the breaking point, he made his way to the shaman's hut to talk to Prentice about the mysterious dog that had appeared earlier that day. Upon knocking on the heavy wooden door, he was invited in by his old friend.

"Well, Stanley," said Prentice, once he had closed the door. "Please have a seat," he said gesturing to the chair by the table.

Stanley took a seat as Prentice took the seat opposite him. The old man stared at him for a few minutes, surveying him without a word. Stanley felt rather awkward and after a continuing silence, he decided to be the one who broke it.

"Prentice, what is this all about?" he pleaded. "What do you know that's not being revealed to me?"

Prentice smiled, which threw Stanley off. He had been expecting some sort of reprimand.

"Stanley, you have a lifetime to learn what this is all about," he said mysteriously. "But I suppose starting from the beginning may be a bit more helpful," he added with a smile.

So Prentice told Stanley the story of his finding. He told him of the dog appearing to Lila and of her adventure through the very same forest he had encountered it, leading to the mountain cave and resulting in his being rescued from starvation and freezing. As Prentice spoke, Stanley was thinking of the mother he could never find. True, Lila had raised him as if she was his mother, but she had told him that his mother had given him up because she couldn't care for him any longer. She had said that one day, he would find her.

Stanley suddenly realized that Prentice had stopped talking and was observing him quietly again.

"Your silence says that things are not in perspective for you yet; am I correct?" he said to Stanley quietly, his elbows resting on the table and his chin in his hands.

"I'm not sure," Stanley said slowly. "I'm not positive how I feel about it all. Truthfully, if I may say, I'm beginning to feel as if I don't belong here."

"Explain," Prentice said, sitting up straighter, his eyes narrowing slightly.

"That's just it — I can't," Stanley said quickly, "but ever since I was a boy, I have often had dreams of faraway lands — lands beyond the walls of these mountains."

"What sort of lands?" said the old man. Stanley could tell that Prentice's curiosity had mounted to its highest, so he eagerly hurried on.

"Well," said Stanley, pulling a concentrated face. "As a child, and even now, most thoughts are of leaving this quiet peaceful valley to explore the land beyond. I dream of far off and unseen beaches or great forests with tree trunks the size of horses, and of deserts that stretch on for miles and miles. It is always moving to me."

Even as he spoke, Stanley saw the beaches, the forests, and the deserts. He felt a strong sense of adventure inside his heart. He wiped a tear from his eye with his arm. He looked up and was once more in the dim light of the hut, staring at Prentice.

"I wasn't fully honest about how I caught that deer," he said, feeling ashamed of himself.

"I must say, I am rather disappointed you concealed something from me," Prentice told Stanley, sounding slightly concerned. "However, I am not surprised."

Stanley felt an uncomfortable heat growing in his body, along with a mixture of guilt and sorrow, much like a child after a scolding.

"I'm sorry," he muttered dully, after a few minutes pause.

Prentice waved his apology away airily with a wrinkled hand.

"Don't be," he said wisely. "Feeling sorry for yourself leads to a path of always losing hope and confidence in yourself and all of your ventures. Eventually, you will lose hope altogether and you will be doomed to a life of failure."

Prentice stared at his pupil for a moment. It was a stern, piercing look. Stanley felt his every pore and movement being read by the old man. Prentice, however, smiled fondly and rose from his chair and walked over to Stanley, bending on a knee so that he was on Stanley's eye level. He clasped his hand around Stanley's shoulders and stared at him with his deep blue eyes.

"That is not the path you are destined for, however," he said in a matter-of-fact tone. "You are destined to succeed in all of your ventures, as well as your life as a whole, even if it's as boring and uneventful as the tale of one of the gardeners' largest pumpkins. The funny thing about it is I was living in this village while the vegetable was being grown. I watched its magnificent progress with my own eyes. Yet, I fear I'm doomed to hear the tale forever."

He looked at Stanley, whose face was blank and his eyebrows were raised. Prentice chuckled heartily.

"Please forgive my rambling, Stanley — rather foolish of me," Prentice said, smiling. "I hereby give you permission to fill me in on what you left out of our previous conversation, which took place earlier this evening."

"Right," said Stanley, determined to sound calm, despite his fear and worry. "I refrained from telling you that the dog . . . well, it talked to me."

Prentice simply looked at him, his smile not fading in the slightest. Stanley was completely confused now.

"I don't understand," he said to his teacher. "Why are you not surprised by this news?"

"Because," Prentice said, casually but seriously, "I was almost certain that if you and the dog ever crossed paths, it would speak to you."

"You were?" Stanley exclaimed offhandedly.

"Yes," replied the shaman quietly, sitting back down in his chair opposite Stanley, as he withdrew a long wooden pipe from his flowing robes and took a long pull on it. He exhaled and watched the progress of the swirling smoke, until it had floated out the window.

"Ever since Lila came to me," said he, as if he had never paused "and told me of a mysterious dog that greatly wanted her attention and her attention alone, I was heavily curious. At first, I thought the dog would speak to her. But that was before she returned from the mountain cave with you in her arms. From that moment on, I was certain that you have been given the gift of Animal Speak. However, the years went by without any sighting of the dog, and I began to lose hope. But two years back, I spotted it. It was just lurking among the wood line, observing you. I knew then that it was only a matter of time. And here we are." He then took another pull from his pipe, as if in victory.

Stanley stared at the shaman, taking in all the information, but not knowing how he felt about it all. It was slightly unnerving to know that Prentice had thought all of this and not once confided it to him.

"Well, what do you propose I do about it?" Stanley said to him, a hint of anger in his voice.

"I am afraid I cannot answer the question you inquire of me," Prentice replied sadly.

"Why not? This isn't fair!" Stanley exclaimed loudly, his anger rising.

"Hold your anger," said Prentice sharply. Power seemed to be emanating from him as he spoke. "I cannot answer your question, my lad, for it is one you must figure out for yourself."

Stanley stared at his mentor with a very dissatisfying look. Prentice however smiled down at him and chuckled.

"If you are unsettled still, talk to Lila," he said, patting

Stanley's shoulder. "But I'm very certain that you should accept this new gift as something grand and fantastic. It shall take you on an amazing journey. I am sure of that."

He stood up and opened his heavy wooden door, letting in the smell of the wood fire crackling in the distance and gestured his pupil out of his hut.

Stanley exited the hut and immediately headed toward Lila's hut. Upon reaching it, he knocked hastily on the wooden door. Lila's face emerged a few moments later, an expression of curiosity on her face.

"What can I do for you, Stanley my dear?" she asked him warmly, beaming and moving aside so he could enter the hut.

There was a merry fire burning in the hearth and a bottle of honey mead on the table. Stanley sat down in a chair at the table as Lila shut the door and sat down opposite him, examining him with soft eyes.

"Did Prentice tell you everything you wished to know?" she asked him fondly.

"Yes, well, most everything," Stanley answered her, sighing sadly. "He didn't tell me what to do next when I asked him."

"Well, I thought that would've been obvious, my dear," she replied, smiling at him.

Stanley had no clue what to say to this, so he remained silent. Lila seemed to know and understand how he was feeling.

"Stanley, you must seek out this animal for yourself," she urged. "I cannot answer that question either, my dear. The only one who can is that dog."

Her voice was stern, and her face had a finalized look to it. Stanley remained silent, staring up at her. Lila smiled and stood up. She walked over to Stanley and put her hands upon his shoulders, looking into his eyes.

"You have a great path ahead of you, my dear," Lila said kindly. "This is your destiny, Stanley. So seek it out and seize it! Let it take you away to wonder and adventure."

Later that night, Stanley was sitting outside his hut by his fireside, smoking from a long wooden pipe that he had carved from a holly tree, trying his best to relax after the day's occurrence of strange events. As he took a small pull, his head swimming with thought, he heard a faint scuffling from the wood line. Turning his head toward the thick trees, he saw a sight that made his heart skip a beat. The dog was sitting by a very large maple tree, and it was staring directly at him! Stanley and the dog stared at each other for at least two hours, neither daring to move. Finally, Stanley stood up, exhausted and drowsy, sleep creeping up on him. He gave one last look at the dog and retreated into his hut to bed. The dog remained watching the hut until the sun began to creep over the mountaintops.

Stanley awoke the next morning to find the dog sitting stock still, right in the doorway of the hut, staring right at him and wagging its tail. Stanley sat up, rubbing his eyes sleepily and yawning heavily. He rested his body against the wall in a comfortable sitting position, looking down at the wagging dog in front of him.

"What is it you want from me?" he asked the creature curiously.

The dog remained silent, continuing to wag its tail furiously. Stanley started feeling annoyed at the dog's stony silence.

"Look," he said to it, wondering if he was going crazy for talking to a dog. "I'm not a big fan of surprises, nor am I very patient; so either tell me what it is you want with me or get stuffed."

"Well that's no way to speak," said the dog smartly. "I was under the impression that you were a pleasant human being."

Stanley nearly fell out of the bed in surprise.

"You . . . you can talk!" he exclaimed, staring at the dog in complete amazement now. "I knew I wasn't imagining it!"

"Yes, I can talk," said the dog sarcastically. "Way to be obvious. Very bright you are."

"Well, what do you want with me?" Stanley asked it, ignoring the dogs snipe at him.

"I want to help you," said the dog seriously. "I am here to guide you and teach you the ways of our people. I have been appointed your guardian since you were born."

"That's rubbish," said Stanley skeptically. "You would be an old and feeble dog by now; how is that possible?"

"An animal that is raised among a family of Speakers remains with that family forever," said the dog.

"I'm afraid I still don't understand," said Stanley, leaning closer now, eager to hear more.

The dog sighed and rolled its eyes.

"Humans and their thirst to know everything," he said. "You really can't accept what's given to you from any source other than yourselves. You must always delve deeper until you pull its very roots up, thus ruining it entirely. Very well, I will explain."

He got up out of the doorway and jumped onto Stanley's bed and sat down, facing him.

"I was found long ago, by a brilliant man — a man who had come from a faraway land known as Elda. I was drowning in a swamp and was only a puppy. This man saved me, and as he spoke to me, I found I could understand his speech. As he nursed me back to health, he told me of the people in his land, how they all could do what he could. We had many adventures together. He eventually met a woman with the same gift, and they had you. But alas, they have both fallen."

"You knew my parents?" Stanley inquired of the dog, amazed.

"Yes," said the dog sadly, "you will know more detail in due time, Stanley."

Stanley looked at the dog. He was intrigued and a little scared at this new gift.

"Who are you?" he asked the dog in wonder.

"My name is Desmond," he said, "and I'm your companion. But more importantly, I'm here to teach you and take you home to be among others like yourself."

"What!" Stanley exclaimed. "I was thinking you'd say 'protect the villagers from harm' or something along those lines."

"These people do not need protecting," said Desmond calmly and quietly. "They have managed to stay hidden from others for ages and ages. Your place lies beyond, Stanley, in Arda — the Speakers Village.

Stanley did not know what think or say but for some odd reason, he felt he could trust Desmond, as if there was a bond, unexplainable and unknown to him until now.

"Fine," he said to Desmond. "Fine, I'll go with you. It's not like I have much of a choice, is it?"

Desmond wagged his tail and licked Stanley's face.

"Not really," said the dog happily. "We'll leave in three weeks."

One week later, Stanley and Desmond were sitting outside their hut, enjoying the beautiful sun and the cool breeze sweeping the valley. Desmond was lying in the grass, basking in the rays of the warm sun, and Stanley was sitting with his back against his hut, smoking from his pipe, his eyes closed.

"I would like to show you part of your history tonight," said Desmond, giving a hearty stretch. Stanley opened his eyes.

"All right, then," he said, looking down at the dog. Stanley had learned throughout the week that he could trust Desmond.

At that very moment, Prentice came striding over to them, his long silky robes billowing in the breeze.

"Hello you two," said the old shaman, bowing low.

"Hello, Prentice," Stanley said getting up, brushing the grass off his own robes. "What can I do for you on a day like this?"

"Well," said Prentice, "I was wondering if you would like to accompany me to my hut, as I have some things for you."

"Of course," Stanley said willingly, and turning to Desmond he said, "Want to come?"

"No," replied Desmond. "I really didn't plan on moving."

"Suit yourself," said Stanley smiling as he followed Prentice toward his hut.

When Stanley and Prentice reached the door of the hut, Prentice pushed it open and beckoned Stanley inside. He closed the door and gestured for Stanley to sit at the table, seating himself at the opposite end. Magical herbs and oils were being burned in a marble bowl that was hovering above a candle on the tabletop. Stanley let the scent of them waft into his nostrils and felt all the stress and anxiety leave his body. He smiled.

"Stanley," said Prentice, addressing his pupil, "I have some items in my possession that I'm sure will aid you on your journey. It is time I passed them on to you."

He reached down by his feet and picked up a rather large, brown hand-woven sack. The sack was packed with bulky, unseen items. Stanley's heart was racing with excitement. The first thing Prentice pulled from the sack was a leather pouch, which was very old indeed and looked as if it had been around the world and back.

"This bag contains magical herbs of my own making called

Lifeleaf," said Prentice, handing him the bag. "Lifeleaf will cure you of most poisons, disease, infection, or sickness. It cannot mend bones, halt bleeding, or stop more serious affairs, however."

"Thank you," Stanley said sincerely, taking the old pouch and feeling it in his hands. He opened it; inside were leaves and flowers of various colors.

"Next," continued Prentice picking up a long and thin, neatly wrapped bundle from the floor, "is this."

He handed the bundle to Stanley who took it with trembling hands. As Stanley took the bundle and as he hastily tore the wrappings away, he saw that it was a beautiful staff of bamboo, bound in red cloth, shimmering jewels dangling on its side. Atop the staff sat a magnificent ruby. Stanley was honored by such a beautiful tool.

"That staff holds the power to wield the elements of the earth around you. Use it wisely, but most importantly, use it carefully," Prentice said sharply to him.

"I will," Stanley said determinately to him.

"Finally, I have a tent made from the strongest vine fibers; it will keep you dry during the harshest of storms."

He then took another bundle from the sack, which was very thin and fragile looking.

"These are the maps of the lands beyond, as far as the Silver City."

Stanley stared at all of this new equipment he was being given by his mentor. He was overcome with gratitude and love.

"I don't know how to thank you enough," he said to Prentice quietly.

"Just do your best to keep out of trouble and don't get yourself killed," said Prentice, smiling down at his pupil with warm sincerity. "You have a great gift, my friend. You have been my best student; to see you grow into a shaman of the earth is all the thanks I need."

He stood up and gestured for Stanley to do the same.

"You are destined for wonder, Stanley," said Prentice and with that, he dismissed Stanley from his hut.

A short time later, Stanley was sitting in his hut stoking the fire, quite full from a magnificent dinner, when in trotted Desmond through the doorway.

"It is time to see what needs to be seen," he told Stanley, looking at him stonily.

"All right, then," said Stanley, getting to his feet and stretching his arms wide. "Just let me get my cloak and staff."

"Very well," said Desmond once Stanley had grabbed his cloak and slung it over his shoulders, his new staff in hand. "Follow me."

He darted through the door and out of sight. Stanley hurried after Desmond, his heart racing. He spotted his friend by the wood line, waiting for him a little ways in by a cluster of spruces. As he approached, Desmond turned away and trotted deeper into the wood. The thick trees seemed to be sucking all light from the sky as Stanley delved on, following his dog. As the two trekked on through the trees' gloomy shadows, the light vanished more and more with each step they took. Before he knew it, Stanley couldn't even see his palm as he waved it blindly in front of his face. He stopped walking abruptly and soon heard Desmond's footsteps falter a moment later.

"What's the matter?" Desmond's voice came from somewhere ahead to his left. "Are you scared of the dark?"

"Don't be stupid," Stanley said irritably through the darkness. "But I would much rather walk with a bit of light than none at all."

Lo and behold! No sooner had the thought left his mouth than the staff gave a mighty, vibrating shudder and burst into a dazzling red light, temporarily blinding them. Blinking rapidly as his eyes adjusted, Stanley could see the massive tree trunks illuminated all around him. He found Desmond a few paces up and hastened to catch up with him.

A few hours later, tired and worn, stopping occasionally to pull bramble and thorns from his cloak, Stanley reached a massive clearing. For the first time in his life, he was gazing up at the Oakhill Mountains. Their summits could not be seen in the darkness of night, and it made Stanley feel very small and miniscule. Looking around, he spotted Desmond sitting at the foot of a rather large cave where a fine stream was rushing out of its mouth toward the wood line and out of sight. Stanley ran over to him, clutching at a stitch in his side, his heart racing through his chest with anticipation. He stared into the dark cave ahead of him.

"What is this place?" he asked Desmond cautiously. The cave had a rather eerie feel to it. Stanley did not like the cold chill emanating from its dark depths.

"This is the place where you were born, my friend, and this is where you will learn about your past," said Desmond firmly to him. "I cannot enter with you, for it is a quest for you, and you alone."

"I understand," said Stanley.

And with a fierce determination, his hands trembling, he entered the cave.

It was wet and gloomy in the cave. The air smelled dry and stale, and it was stiflingly humid. His staff gave him enough light to see the narrow cave walls. There was no escaping the water, however; the current grew stronger with each splashy step he took, soaking his feet and sending chills up his spine, making him shiver violently. He could hear a dripping ahead of him, growing louder as he made his way on through the cave, and he knew he must be close. He was right. Around the corner, he came upon an opening revealing a large cavern, a gloomy pool in its center, glowing red in the dim light of his staff. As he approached the pool, he caught sight of a dark shape lying a few feet away from its edge, and he felt his heart drop. There, lying on the cave's cold, damp floor was the skeleton of a woman. His mother — he knew it must be. There was no doubt in his heart.

Quite suddenly, the surface of the pool began to ripple violently. Stanley knelt down and stared into the water. Images began to swirl on its surface now, the clear water no longer rippling.

He was now looking down at the outside of the mountain, showing the outside of the very cave he was kneeling in. sunlight was dazzling the land about, as a woman carrying a bundle of blankets came trotting out of the wood line, a dog close at her heels. The woman looked exhausted as she ran to the cave. The water rippled again, and the scene changed. The woman was lying on the cave's floor now, in the same spot she was presently in. She was holding a small child in her arms, and the dog was sitting next to them, whining. The woman looked over to the dog and raised a shaky hand to pat its head, her fingers stroking its soft ears.

"Desmond," she whispered to it, "Desmond . . ." Her voice was pained and hurt, but soft and gentle. "I'm dying, Desmond. You . . . you must save my child, Desmond. Protect him from harm; teach him our ways when he is ready. He is the one who will bring peace to our people. This I know. Protect him, Desmond; be his guardian . . . his . . . animal."

She closed her eyes with a smile and died right there on the cold cave floor. The pool rippled once more, revealing Lila exiting the cave, carrying baby Stanley in her arms. The pool rippled and once again was normal.

When Stanley had hurriedly left the cave, he found Desmond waiting for him at the wood line. He made his way over to him and stooped down and scratched him behind his ears. Desmond wagged his tail happily.

"Thank you," Stanley said simply to him.

"Let us get back to the village before it gets too late," said Desmond and with a mighty bound, he led Stanley off into the trees. The pair disappeared in the thickness, making their way home together.

Chapter Three: The Departure

A few days before his departure, Stanley began to notice a drastic change in the villagers' attitude toward him. It had turned very uncomfortable and nasty for Stanley. The villagers would no longer sit with him at mealtimes, leaving him and Desmond to sit alone with Lila and Prentice. They also refrained from sitting by the fireside circle at night and listening to his plans for his adventure into the lands beyond, thus forcing Stanley to make his plans in his hut in isolation and solitude. They gathered in groups during the day, talking in hurried, whispered voices, stopping abruptly when they caught sight of him or Desmond.

It made Stanley sick to see such intolerance; he had thought he knew these people. Hadn't he spent his whole life among them, growing and learning with their care and nourishment? Why were the people he loved and cared for treating him like an outsider? When Stanley expressed his feelings to Prentice and Lila, he did not get the answers he had hoped for.

Lila simply smiled warmly at him.

"This is simply the way of them coping with your leave, dear. Simply the sad knowledge of someone that they love and respect leaving. All of these feelings are mixed with slight jealousy at your newfound gift. Give them time; they will grow to regret their actions."

Stanley highly doubted this.

Prentice sighed deeply and replied wisely.

"You must learn to accept that some men are cruel for no reason whatsoever, and that by using your most powerful weapon of all, can you defeat them."

"And what — may I ask — is my greatest weapon?" Stanley asked skeptically.

"Your heart, my friend," said Prentice firmly. "Your love and kindness, the love you hold for all that is good."

Stanley really couldn't see how he could ignore the villagers' actions, and pretend like everything was fine and dandy. And he sure wasn't going to accept that this was just an act of sadness at his leaving, either. As far as Stanley was concerned, the sooner they departed the better. But Desmond wouldn't allow this.

"We still have a good deal to do before we depart," said the dog anxiously. "To leave now would be highly irrational, not to mention extremely foolhardy."

So Stanley had retreated into the woods every day for the last week now and today found him sitting comfortably with his back against a tree, far from the villagers' whispers and meddlesome prying eyes. Desmond was lying on his belly by Stanley's feet, his mighty legs stretched out in full, rolling occasionally on the soft mossy earth. Stanley was observing some maps he had laid out next to him, preparing himself for the approaching adventure and marking out their trail. The departure was tomorrow morning, and Stanley had never felt so anxious in his life. He was wondering to himself if he would ever return to this place and if he would even make it to his destination, because the way Desmond had explained it, it sounded near impossible.

Their road would lead them north to northwest at first, through the treacherous mountains surrounding Oakhill. Once out of the mountains, the companions would make their way north, through the Four Rock Plains. The plains were well known to be the main hunting grounds for the mountain lions, which dwelled on their outskirts. This scrap of information did not comfort Stanley at all. If they made it all the way north out of the plains, they would then come upon the mighty Deepwood Forest, an almost impassable fortress of thick, massive, redwood-sized trees. The forest was rumored to house many evils as well, for the shadow that loomed around the forest and inside of it was the most unpleasant imaginable. Stories had been told to Stanley by Prentice of dark whispers when travelers entered the forest, following them, making them go off the path, only to come to their deaths from being hungry and lost. They decided they would worry about making it out of the Deepwood alive, then focus on the rest of the journey, which would take them southwest through the Oxen Fields and finally into the Speakers village of Arda.

"Our main focus, however, is making it through the mountains and across the plains at a good pace," Desmond said. "From there, we will deal with the path ahead."

"Right," Stanley replied. "How long does it take to get to Arda from here?" he added as an afterthought.

"If our luck holds out and the path is free of dangers, then I would say about a week, but we mustn't depend on that happening. I foresee the Deepwood slowing us down. I will say no more," he replied sullenly.

Stanley's heart dropped slightly at these words, though he didn't express his feelings to Desmond. He was too anxious at the moment to let it bother him. Desmond said they'd worry about the forest when they got to it, and that was what he was going to do.

Later that day, Stanley and Desmond returned to the village, their spirits full and their hopes high. The second they entered the sight of the villagers, however, Stanley's heart sank. Upon seeing the two returning, the villagers closest to them dropped what they were doing and took off in separate directions, toward their huts, snapping their doors harshly as they walked by. Stanley did all he could to ignore them as he made his way to his hut, pretending not to notice their eyes peering at them through their veiled windows. He reached his hut and as he and Desmond entered, he slammed the door shut, leaving them in a dim light due to the now fading daylight. He sat down on his bed and put his head into his hands, sighing slightly. He lifted his head and addressed Desmond to take his mind off the villagers.

"How do animals choose their humans?" he said curiously.

Desmond stared at him for a few seconds before replying.

"It is not entirely up to the animal to choose the human," he said quietly.

"Why?" asked Stanley.

"The human must seek us out as well," he said simply.

"I don't understand," Stanley said, altogether confused. "Don't animals have instincts more acute than those of a human? Can't they tell when they find the Speaker?"

"We only reveal ourselves to the person that we know needs us," Desmond said shortly. "In some cases, an animal will spend its entire life searching for their counterpart, but it may never find it."

Stanley stared out of his window into the trees lining the

village and the lands beyond, his mind wandering to all of the animals in the world searching for their whole lives for a human they may never find. He suddenly had an urge to help them all.

"If only my hut was bigger," he said to himself.

Desmond laughed, wagging his tail.

"You will do and accomplish many extraordinary things, my friend," the dog said to him kindly.

"No," said Stanley, correcting him. "We will do extraordinary things."

"Also," Desmond added, as if struck by a sudden afterthought, "I've come to notice that you are not a very capable hunter. I can help with that."

Stanley laughed heavily, more than he had laughed in quite some time. He leaned down to scratch Desmond's head.

"Yeah, I suppose you will," he said, grinning.

Later that night, Stanley once again found himself sitting alone at the far end of the feast table, Desmond lying quietly by his feet. To tell the truth, he really didn't mind much now. No matter how much the villagers taunted him and made him feel uncomfortable, he was determined to enjoy the last proper meal he would have for who knows how long. The table was creaking with the weight of the food. There was fish, venison, seed cakes, bread, milk, clover honey, ham, and lots of wine, mead, and ale. As Stanley quietly enjoyed these delicacies, the villagers would look down the table and give him dark looks.

When the feast was finished, the villagers gathered around the fire and told stories for a change. They told the story of the giants coming in from the west and creating the Four Rock Plains. Stanley, who was sitting a short way away, near the feast table, noticed the villagers left out the tale of Animal Speak, which was a usual favorite of the village as a whole. A few hours later, the crowd returned to their huts with dreaming on their minds, leaving only the hunters sitting at the table, drinking heavily. This was a usual occurrence, as the hunters were the first to rise and the last to go to sleep at night. After sitting a few moments in the quiet, Stanley was able to overhear a few parts of the conversation, and with a gut sinking pang, he realized they were talking about him.

"Do you think he'll make it through the mountains?" one of the men said to his counterpart.

"If you ask me," said the man, "he won't get far. He either is going to fall to his death on those mountain cliffs, or if he does make it through, the lions will get him for sure."

"What about the dog? What about the gift?" said another.

"Bah!" said the second man. "It's all a lie, a plea for attention, rubbish."

"Agreed," said the first man. "He'll never survive it. He's a goner."

All the men laughed nastily. Stanley stood up, fury raging in him; he'd had enough of this nonsense — this stupid and petty behavior. The men jumped; none of them were aware of Stanley listening.

"So," began Stanley, his voice shaking from the anger bubbling up inside of him. "You all think I'm mad, don't you? You think I'm crazy. Let me tell you something. I'm not mad or crazy. I intend to make it all the way to my destination, and three drunken hunters won't persuade me otherwise."

The three men rose to their feet at once, as did Desmond. Desmond growled deeply and bared his teeth at them, his fur raised on his back. The men eyed Desmond for a moment, but did nothing more. They sat back down looking slightly defeated. The closest addressed Stanley in a pleading voice.

"Stanley, I've known you me whole life, and I got to say: you're not a great hunter, mate. How do you expect to make it? We are just asking you to spare us all the trouble of going to retrieve you when you get lost."

"You think I asked for any of this?" Stanley bellowed at them. "I didn't ask for it, but I was chosen, and I'm going to go through with it, no matter where it leads me. You are too close-minded to realize that there is much more out there than this valley, and it's waiting to be explored."

Stanley turned on his heel and headed toward the hut, ignoring the villagers who had poked their heads out of their doorways, Desmond trotting along at his side. Once inside his hut, he slammed his door hard and addressed Desmond.

"I'm not waiting anymore; we're leaving tonight," he said firmly.

"Agreed," said Desmond. "Make haste, pack all you need, and tell no one. We leave in an hour."

An hour later, Stanley stood in the center of his hut with his pack on his back, fully loaded with tools, food, supplies, maps, and any other paraphernalia he might need. A long black traveling cloak was draped over his shoulders, his staff was in his hand, and a messenger bag full of medicines and herbs was hanging off his side. He turned to face Desmond, who was sitting quietly in the doorway.

"Are you ready?" inquired Desmond, getting up and stretching.

"Yes," said Stanley simply.

"Very well, let's get going then."

Without a sound, they left the hut and headed toward the wood line. Not a soul heard or saw them going into the darkness. The villagers would wake the next morning to find the hut abandoned with no trace left of Stanley. Just before vanishing into the trees, Stanley looked back at the quiet, sleeping village and wondered if he would ever see it again.

The two travelers made their way through the forest, Stanley's staff lighting the way through the brambles and thickets strewn about the mossy wood floor. Neither said much, for the effort it took to get through the forest was most exhausting. Hours and hours they journeyed, until they reached the cave where Stanley was born. Stanley stopped, staring into the cave's dark depths.

"Wait here," he said to Desmond.

Leaving Desmond sitting by his pack, he entered the cave. He wound his way into the cavern where his mother was lying by the surface of the underwater pool. He stooped down and removed his cloak, wrapping his mother's body in it with extreme care. He picked up the bundled body and carried it out of the cave to the place where Desmond sat next to his pack. Stanley opened his pack and withdrew a shovel from it with much difficulty, owing to the bag's girth. Immediately, he began to dig. Desmond stared quietly at his companion for a minute or two, and then began to dig himself, his paws working furiously, throwing earth in all directions. Hours passed, but the man and his dog continued to dig, knowing that with each patch of dirt thrown over the body, it would be more at peace. When they were finished, Stanley got up and mopped his brow with his sleeve, looking down at the now smoothly packed earth. The sun had begun to rise over the peaks of the mountains, throwing dazzling rays in all directions. He looked at Desmond.

"Well," he said, "let's get to the top of the mountains before nightfall then."

"Very well," said Desmond wagging his tail.

And sniffing the air as he went, Desmond led the way to a rather narrow, rocky path heading up into the ominous mountains.

Chapter Four: Elliot

Morning crept up on the travelers slowly as they made their way up the path. The morning dew was now glistening on the grass and rocks on the mountain's path, making it slippery and dangerous. Desmond had said the path led north, up through the mountains to the very summits. Once at the top, they would make their way west on the summit path that eventually wound down through the other side of the mountains, to the plains below.

Stanley had predicted the path would be no easy feat, and he was quite right. The path twisted and turned, winding its way up and up. All the while, the path seemed to be shrinking as they climbed, forcing them to walk in single file, with Desmond leading the way up. There were a few occasions where Stanley nearly lost his footing, slipping on the rocks that were coming loose from his weight. Quite suddenly, they came upon a cliff, and about ten feet in front of them was the path, once again wide enough for them to walk side by side with space to spare. The only problem was: how were they going to get across to the other side?

"I didn't pack any rope," said Stanley. "Didn't think it was necessary — just goes to show, doesn't it?"

Desmond turned around and headed down the path, going about twenty feet before turning back around.

"Wha—" Stanley began, but before he could finish, Desmond had broken into a full pace run toward the cliff.

With one mighty leap, he cleared the treacherous gap, and his paws landed softly on the rocky path ahead. He turned to face Stanley, who was staring open-mouthed at the dog.

"Your turn," Desmond said to him.

"No way, mate. You are crazy if you think I'll make that jump. Absolutely not," exclaimed Stanley.

"Well then, use your human intelligence to fly across," said

Desmond sarcastically.

Grumbling, Stanley tossed his pack and other belongings across the cliff's gap, so that they thudded gently on the path ahead. He gave himself plenty of running space; if he didn't clear the gap in one jump, he would fall to the rocky bottom below. He bolted up the path toward the cliff's edge and gave a mighty leap. He soared in midair for a few seconds, and then came to clumsily land on the path ahead, falling onto his pack and crashing into the rocky ground.

"Looks like you were able to make the jump after all," said Desmond wagging his tail as Stanley stood up and brushed pebbles and dirt off himself.

"Yeah, very funny," said Stanley darkly, retrieving his pack from the ground and slinging it over his shoulder. "Let's keep moving."

They continued on their way. On and on the path led them. Up, up, up, they climbed, seeing nothing but a massive wall of rock on either side of them. Stanley was in pain now, his muscles aching from the excruciating uphill climb. He was quite sure his legs would give out any minute, leaving him to collapse upon the path. Even Desmond was beginning to feel weary. He was panting heavily, and he had slowed his pace to a slow trot, so that he was only a little way head of Stanley. Finally, after what felt like ages to Stanley, the sun began to set and the two companions met level ground. Stanley looked around and gasped, completely amazed at what he saw.

They were standing on the very summit of the mountain, looking out at the lands beyond. Standing upon the summit was a lone tree to the left of which, there lay a path. The path was the only way down the mountains. Desmond said it wound down for miles into the massive plains below. Looking off the edge of the cliffside into the plains, Stanley saw four massive rocks set across their landscape. Beyond the plains, there was a black mass of trees that went on into the horizon and out of sight: the Deepwood Forest. With a small pang of fear, he remembered that this was their road. He heard the screech of a falcon in the distance and looked up to see it soaring high above him, circling something unseen. He watched it for few minutes until it had disappeared from view.

They set up camp on the summit; the tent Prentice had given him was sitting peacefully under the tree. There was a warm fire roaring and a beautiful view. Stanley looked out at the sky, now growing dim as the night drew in. Desmond had ventured down the path and had managed to catch a squirrel for dinner. The squirrel was roasting heartily on the fire, and a pot of water was boiling a stew of herbs and spices. It wasn't much, but at least it was a warm meal. Once Stanley finished his supper, he retreated to his tent and lay down, quite calm and very relaxed. The tent flap was open, revealing the lands about, and a most breathtaking night's sky, the billions of stars above twinkling and shimmering behind a beautiful, gleaming quarter moon. Stanley felt his eyelids growing heavy, and the urge to sleep slowly crept up on him. He closed his eyes, smiling to himself a little, fell off into a blissful sleep, and did not wake for some time.

When he did come to, he could tell it was still dark. Desmond was nowhere inside the tent. As Stanley rolled over and closed his eyes, he thought he could hear a faint scuffling coming from outside. Thinking it was only Desmond, he drifted back off to sleep, just as a falcon gave a quiet screech from the tree above him.

Stanley awoke quite suddenly the next morning. The sun's rays were shining into the tent, blinding him. He hastily closed the flap, which he had neglected to do the night before, and began to dress. He was fastening his cloak when he heard an unfamiliar voice address Desmond, coming from outside.

"Would you like a sausage, Des?" the voice asked the dog.

"Yes, please," Desmond's replied.

Stanley bolted out of the tent, forgetting that it was only feet away from the cliff. The bright sun hit his eyes as he burst out of the tent, once again blinding him from lack of adjusting. Without a warning, his left foot slipped off the edge of the cliff. Stanley would have died if it hadn't been for the stranger. The man jumped up and raced toward Stanley before he had slipped, stuck out his hand and grasped Stanley's shoulder, pulling him back to safety.

"Steady on, brother," said the voice sounding amused. "God, man, didn't anyone tell you not to place your tent opening next to a cliff. You almost died without breakfast; what an awful morning that would have been."

Stanley stood up, his eyes now adjusting to the light. He took in the stranger, who was now smiling at him. He was wearing a dirty, very worn and tattered cloak, which was amber in color, or at least that was its color now. His hood was down, revealing a tangle of brown hair that almost fell to his shoulders. His face was lined and worn as much as the cloak, but it was kind. The man looked as if he had been through a lifetime in only a few years. His shoulders were broad, and he had strong powerfully built arms. He wore a black tunic which was nearly as dirty as the cloak, and black trousers that were tucked into thick brown boots. A sword was dangling in its sheath on his left leg, its hilt gleaming in the bright sun. A traveling bag was lying next to some blankets sitting a little way from the fire, which was sending the smell of sausages into the air.

"Name's Elliot, brother," said the man, stretching out his hand to Stanley in greeting.

"Stanley," he replied, taking Elliot's hand and shaking it. "I take it that was you I heard scuffling around last night, then?"

"Aye," said Elliot, sitting back down by the fire and ladling a few sausages onto a plate and handing it to Stanley.

Stanley sat down and happily ate his sausages as Elliot talked.

"Sorry about the noise," he said. "I hope I didn't keep you up too long."

"S'alrigh—" Stanley said, his mouth full of sausage.

"I came up here early morning; Oliver told me there was a camp up here. I came to check it out, thinking you might be some of the men from the west," he told them as they ate. "When I reached the path leading up here, I met your dog, Desmond. He was a little wary of me at first, but realizing what I was, he warmed up very quickly."

Elliot scratched Desmond behind the ears.

"What do you mean?" asked Stanley, bemused. "He realized what you were?"

Elliot stared at him a moment before he answered, a curious look on his face.

"I'm a Speaker like you, mate."

"What?" Stanley exclaimed. "You speak it, too?"

"Aye," said Elliot. "Ever since I was a lad when me father passed on, Oliver's been a great friend and guardian to me."

"Oliver?" asked Stanley.

"Me animal o' course," he said.

Stanley looked around, but saw no animal anywhere.

"Where —?" began Stanley, but at that moment, there was loud bark from the path ahead, and Desmond came bounding up, his tail wagging furiously. There was a screech from above, and Stanley looked up to see a rather large and grand looking falcon soaring high above, circling its way down to meet them. The falcon had black and white wings and a brown speckled body. It soared down gracefully to them and came to rest upon Elliot's shoulder. The bird, like its master, had a worn but powerful look about him. He cocked his head slightly to the side, looking at Stanley. He spoke in a soft voice, almost a whisper.

"Hello, Stanley," it said to him. "It is a great pleasure to meet you. Desmond has told me much about you."

"The pleasure is all mine," said Stanley, stroking the bird's soft plumage.

"This is Oliver," said Elliot. "This bird and I have seen many adventures together, some more dangerous than others. We've been friends for a very long time.

They then all sat down and ate some breakfast. As Stanley ate, he felt his insides warming. It was a good feeling to know that there were others like him in the world. It was wonderful to know he wasn't alone, and he told this to Elliot.

"Cheers, brother," said Elliot smiling at him. Then becoming a little more serious, he said, "So, Desmond tells me that you lot are headed for the Deepwood Forest."

"Yes," said Stanley, "that is our road."

"Well you're going mad if you think you'll make it through alone," he said darkly. "That forest is evil, mate; strange things lurk in the darkness there. Things that will haunt your dreams forevermore ..." He shuddered.

"I'm coming with you," he said finally.

Stanley grinned at Elliot, and Desmond barked happily.

"Now that we are all acquainted and full of food, I think it's best if we move on," said Desmond wisely.

"I agree with that notion," replied Stanley.

They packed up the tent and all of their provisions, and within no time, all four travelers were ready to depart the mountain summit. The road down the mountain was a merry one. For the first few hours, everything was perfect. The company laughed and sang together, taking in the beautiful countryside beyond, the sun shining warm above them. Then without a warning, the road grew very steep, and they had to focus all of their energy to get down safely. The rocks were very loose as they walked along, and they had to be careful about where they stepped. Finally, after much grumbling and effort, when the sun had disappeared from view revealing the moon and galaxies above them, they reached the bottom of the mountains.

Their eyes now saw the massive plains, stretching on forever in the darkness, and the massive rocks throwing nearly everything in shadows. Just beyond their vision was the Deepwood Forest, waiting silently for them. Stanley shuddered.

"Stanley," said Elliot from behind him, making him jump. "Let's set up camp here tonight. We will cross the plains in the morning. It should take us nearly a day I think."

"Right," replied Stanley, starting to unpack his bag.

Elliot started a fire and Desmond and Oliver went off to hunt. Oliver said the best they would probably do would be a handful of field mice because the mountain lions claimed the plains as their hunting grounds, and it was not a good idea to get in their way.

Later on, a blazing fire was warming them comfortably after their long, exhausting trudge down the mountains. A little later after the fire started, a large fat groundhog was roasting on its flames. After their dinner, the company sat around the fire, Stanley and Elliot smoking their pipes, watching their smoke rings swirling away into the starry sky. After a while, growing tired and weary, they retreated into their beds. As Stanley lay down in his tent, Desmond curling up by his feet, he heard Elliot talking to Oliver.

"It's an awful sight nicer now, having another around, eh?" he asked the falcon.

"Aye," replied the bird.

With that, Stanley drifted off to sleep, smiling.

Chapter Five: Weather and Woods

The next morning, the group of travelers awoke to a particularly violent storm. As they hurriedly packed the tent and their belongings, the thunder clapped and the lightning flashed above them. The rain flowed fast and heavy as it beat down on them, soaking them to their skin.

The way across the plains was long, miserable, and considerably wet. They trudged through the storm until midday; the wind was so heavy that Oliver could not fly. He sat perched on Elliot's shoulder, occasionally being thrown off by a violent gust of wind. They stopped to unpack the tent (which was completely dry) and ate lunch. Elliot had made a fire, much to Stanley's surprise. He said he could make a fire anywhere, in any weather, and he had been quite right. They cheered up a little bit as they sat huddled in the tent, drying off some and sipping on hot soup. They decided that they would remain where they were until the next morning. Elliot had told them that the forest was only a few hours distance, so there was really no point getting soaked all over again.

"Hopefully, the storm will have died out by morning," he said to them all, crammed in the tent. "We have to ration our provisions and be very careful from now on. There's not much that is good to eat in the forest, and there's hardly any water."

"Where is the forest entrance?" Stanley asked him curiously.

"Well," said Elliot, thinking hard. "There's a path not far from here, to the east. We should reach it by noon, which is good. The forest is uncommonly dark at all times of the day; reaching it then will give us maximum visibility."

As the storm raged on, pounding down upon the lands about,

the four travelers sat in their tent, laughing and joking together. They were all waiting for the miserable rain to pass, but very happy to be warm and dry. As they drifted off into uncomfortable dreams, Stanley thought he heard the cry of a lion in the distance.

The next morning, they awoke to several things. First, they noticed that the rain hadn't let off much. Secondly, there was a lion's head poking in through the tent. Elliot gave a yell, followed by a mighty leap into the beast, knocking it out of the tent. In his haste, however, he managed to knock over the pole holding up their tent, causing its collapse onto Stanley, Oliver, and Desmond. When they untangled themselves from the heavy canvas, they saw through the pounding rain that they were surrounded by four lions. The lions were baring their teeth and growling deeply at them, circling them like cornered prey. The fifth lion in the group was in a furious wrestling match with Elliot. Oliver was squawking madly above them, soaring down upon the lion and tearing into it with his talons. Desmond was standing in front of Stanley, growling and barking viciously, his hair on end. Stanley's staff was in his hand, and as he brandished it at the lions, a strange whistling was emanating from it, as if it was sucking in the wind from around them.

The lions surrounding the company were closing in now. The lion closest to them, his mane dripping with rain, spoke to Stanley.

"You have lost, humans," it said in a low growl, grinning and revealing long, sharp fangs. "Dispose of your weapons and prepare to suffer our wrath."

"You will have to go through all of us!" Stanley bellowed, sounding braver than he felt.

The lions all gave hideously evil laughs at these words.

"Very well, you will meet death by our doing."

Suddenly, Elliot had broken free from his wrestling match with the lion. He gave a mighty kick at the beast, knocking it to the ground, rolling. It jumped up and pounced at Elliot, its claws outstretched, ready to rip him apart. But Elliot was too fast. He grabbed a boomerang from within his tunic and threw it with all his might at the lion. With perfect precision, the boomerang spun into the air and soared toward the lion. A second later, the lion had thudded to the ground, dead. Elliot had decapitated it. He turned toward the other lions, his sword raised.

"You'd be wise to leave now, unless you fancy your 'eads on the ground as well."

The lion that had been taunting Stanley gave a roar of fury.

"Filthy human, it is now time to die!"

The lions sprung at their prey. Without any warning, the wind collecting in Stanley's staff released itself. A large stream issued out of the tip and shot straight into the air, and then it rounded on the attackers. The force was incredible! Like a hurricane, the wind picked up all of the lions right off the ground and threw them fifty feet into the distance. They could hear them yelping and howling as they rolled away from vision. Stanley and Elliot let out a laugh together.

"You shouldn't have done that," Desmond said quietly to them both.

"Well, I'm glad he did," said Elliot, looking ecstatic, even though the rain had soaked them to the bone yet again. Patting Stanley on his shoulder, he said, "We would all be dead now if he hadn't. Cheers mate."

"We must hurry on," he said, ignoring Elliot, his voice anxious and tense. "They will be back for sure, and there will be more of them. We must be far away from this place."

So the company hastily threw their things into their packs and set off immediately. After about half an hour of trudging through the rain, they reached the forest. The trees were black and dark looking, and they were nearly as tall as redwoods. The rain clouds looming above gave it a more menacing look than Stanley could ever have imagined. To the left was a very large opening and a path leading into the trees. The lower branches formed a sort of arch over the path. The path itself was nearly pitch black, and what was worse, they had no idea if it would lead them to the other side. The more Stanley stared into the trees' dark depths, the less he wanted to enter. The forest itself was giving him a very foreboding feeling, and its branches and thicket were so heavy, it seemed to create a void. As for visibility, they could see no more than twenty or so feet ahead of them.

"Well there's no point standing here staring at it," said Elliot, making them all jump. "We have two choices, the first being to go in the forest and hope our luck holds out. The other choice is to sit here and wait for those lions to find us. Personally, I choose life."

They, of course, saw the logic in this.

"You're right," said Stanley. "We go in now, or not at all."

So the four travelers entered the dark abysmal forest. Almost at once, they were thrown into complete darkness. All that could be heard was the crunching of their feet on the forest floor, and the soft *plunk, plunk* of the raindrops on the enormous canopy of trees. Elliot lit a torch, and light surrounded them, but almost immediately the torch gave a hiss and had extinguished itself.

"Wh—" began Elliot, but he did not finish.

A shrill giggle issued from somewhere in the darkness.

"Who's there?" Stanley bellowed into the darkness, but no answer came.

They stood there, rooted to the spot, silently listening. Stanley gave a roar of frustration and knocked his staff against a tree. Light burst from the tip, sending the forest into a bright red glow, momentarily blinding them.

"Well that's clever," said Elliot.

As they made their way through the path, Stanley had an inkling that they were going in circles. The path did not seem to have an end as they trudged on for hours, tired and hungry, feeling like they had been going for days. There was no sunlight to guide the travelers, only the sound of rain. The path was like a road of everlasting night, going on forever and ever. After stumbling clumsily through the semi-darkness for nearly a day's length, they decided to halt for the evening.

They set up the tent but could not get a fire going, no matter how hard Elliot tried. Stanley even attempted using his staff, but there was some magic in the forest that was preventing it. So, after a cold supper, they decided it was time to retire to their beds. Elliot suggested that they post a guard throughout the night in shifts. Stanley was the first watchman.

He sat down at the mouth of the tent, staring blindly into the blackness, wondering if he would ever see the stars or moon again. Would he be lost forever in the darkness, searching for a way out? For hours, all was still and silent in the dim glow of his staff. Suddenly, Stanley thought he heard a strange whispering coming from the depths of the blackness. Was he just hearing voices? Or was someone out there, just beyond the range of his vision, watching him silently?

Then out of the darkness came the shrill giggle again. Stanley shuddered. He stood up, gripping his staff tightly. His staff began to grow brighter, as if it knew Stanley need more light. Stanley was about to start heading toward the source of the sound when Elliot emerged from the tent, pulling on his cloak. Oliver perched on his shoulder.

"Stanley?" he said, with a tired yawn, "where were you off to, brother?"

"I was about to look for the source of the strange sounds," he replied firmly.

"You don't wanna do that, mate," said Elliot walking over to him and staring into the trees. "You would be lost come morning — or worse."

Stanley continued to stare into the darkness. He could've sworn he saw a large shadow moving through the trees. Elliot placed his hand on his shoulder, making him jump; he had completely forgotten that he was standing right next to him.

"You need rest, brother," he said, staring at Stanley with a piercing look. "Go on into the tent to bed before this wood muddles your wits."

Defeated by reason, Stanley retreated into the tent where Desmond was curled up in a ball by his pillow. Within minutes of lying down on the soft earth, he had drifted off to sleep. The whispering and giggling were out of his mind.

The next day, Stanley had remembered the feeling that they were going in circles. Today was different, however. As they traveled along, he had the odd feeling that they were being followed. They bumbled along through on their second day in the forest even more tired than the day before, if that was possible. Stanley would see eyes watching him through the trees, blinking back at him silently when he made contact with them. Every time he rushed toward them to get a closer look, they would vanish.

There were a few things that had changed notably on their second day. The morning gave them a good feeling, as it was rain free. To their astonishment, they were able to start a fire at lunchtime, and feasted on a few rabbits that Oliver had procured the night before while on guard duty with Elliot. They continued on their way after lunch, knowing that they may well be out of food by the next morning, despite their careful rationing. Then, out of the trees, the shrill giggle rang out once more, making the travelers freeze in their tracks, rooted to the spot with fear. Desmond began to bark loudly, but he was cut off by a woman's voice, issuing from the tress.

"Keep on the right path at the fork; the left will lead you to your doom."

"Who's there?" Stanley yelled back toward the spot where the voice came from.

There was no answer, only silence. After a minute or two, Elliot spoke.

"What on earth was all of that about?" he asked Stanley curiously, surveying him as he spoke.

"That—" said Stanley, now moving up the path at a quicker pace, determined to find the voice. "That is what I've been hearing ever since we arrived in this damn wood."

"Well that's just grand," said Elliot darkly.

"Brilliant," squawked Oliver.

"Wonderful," said Desmond.

Stanley ignored all of them.

"I don't suppose you know what to make of it, brother?" said Elliot to him.

"No idea," Stanley grumbled.

After nearly running for some time, Stanley slowed his pace and accepted defeat. The travelers drove on a few more hours until Desmond, who had taken the lead, stopped suddenly. They had reached a fork in the path: one way winding left, the other twisting off to the right. Elliot was staring at the paths curiously, and then he burst out, his voice hurried and excited.

"Wait a moment," he said to them. "The voice told us to go right, so I think we should. I believe it may be trying to help us."

"Are you mad?" Stanley bellowed. "What if whoever or whatever is out there is just trying to lead us to a trap?"

"If it wanted to kill us," Elliot said thoughtfully, "I think it would have done so by now."

Stanley looked at his new friend, amazed at this bit of bravery and daring.

"Fine," he replied finally, "but you lead the way."

So Elliot led the way through the path that led to the right, walking in single file. He held a torch in his left hand, lighting their way through the dimness. As the night crept up on them, the stars were beginning to twinkle in through the thinner leaves. They had reached the heart of the forest. They set up camp next to a small stream that was set by the path. They finished the last of the rabbit on the fire they had built. They set up the tent next to a clump of blueberry bushes, which they gathered for the next day, occasionally munching on one right from the vine. As the company laughed by the fire, Stanley and Elliot smoking their pipes, they felt as if they would be all right after all. Stanley drifted off into a deep uninterrupted sleep in his tent that night. He had dreams of thunderous footfalls, giggling, whispers, and the growls of a bear.

The next morning, when Stanley awoke, the sun was shining bright in his eyes, nearly blinding him as he opened them. He blinked. With a gut-wrenching pang, he realized that he was not where he had been when he had fallen asleep. He had been moved, and he was completely alone.

Chapter Six: Lumen

Stanley blinked again and rolled over. Immediately, he was falling through the air, down to the ground, an occasional branch hitting him in the face. With a sickening *crunch*, he landed on his right arm. Judging by the pain in his arm, Stanley was sure it was broken now. He stood up, wincing as he did so, taking in his surroundings.

He was standing atop a grassy hill with a large willow tree perched on its top, its leaves flowing softly in the wind. The hill itself was set in the corner of a large grassy clearing. In the center of the clearing was a shallow pool, rocks surrounding the borders of it, as if they had been placed there purposefully. A stream was issuing out of one side of the pool, flowing in from the dark trees beyond. A path was set a few feet from the stream and there was another path near the hill.

Stanley stood for a few minutes, rubbing his injured arm and debating which path would lead him back to his friends, if they were still where they were supposed to be, when a soft voice spoke from behind him, making him jump.

"Hello. My name is Lumen. Are you okay?" it asked Stanley curiously.

Stanley winced with pain as he turned to take in the mysterious speaker. He was staring at a woman, and not just any woman. Stanley knew from the second he laid his eyes on her, that there was something remarkable about her. She had flowing blonde hair that shined like summer; atop her head she had placed a crown of flowers. She wore a dress of most interesting design; it seemed to be made with lily pads and forest leaves that were the colors of fall. She had eyes that were as green as the greenest grass. Slung across her shoulders was a quiver of arrows and a bow made of birch. Stanley thought she looked as if she had been made from all the seasons of the world.

"Er, sorry, but who are you? And where are my friends?"

Stanley said to the woman, somewhat awkwardly.

"My name is Lumen," she repeated again, then added, "Is your arm okay? It looks broken."

"Yeah, it is," Stanley said to her with a dark look. "No thanks to you."

"Well if you hadn't fallen out of my tree, that wouldn't have been a problem," she retorted back calmly.

"I would never have fallen if I had never been placed there from the start," Stanley said heatedly. "And where are my friends?" he inquired of her once more.

"They are fine," she said simply to him, smiling a little. "They are gathering food in the forest. Everything is fine."

"Why did you put me in the tree?" he asked her, a little calmer now. He did not understand why, but he trusted Lumen.

"I thought you enjoyed nature, being a shaman and all that. So naturally, waking up in a tree would be ideal. For one thing, you are far from the reach of predators. And trees are just relaxing things to be in, generally. I guess I was wrong." She sighed deeply and looked at Stanley's arm. "Let me get you some wrappings for that arm, then."

She hopped down right off the hill and out of view. A moment later, she had reappeared with a sling and some wrappings.

"Sit," she said happily, pushing him down and making him sit.

As she wrapped his arm up, she hummed quietly to herself. Stanley had no idea what to make of this odd woman. He had no idea how someone could possibly be this happy in a place so obviously miserable.

"Do you live here?" he asked her. "Here in the forest?"

"Oh, yes," Lumen replied happily. "This is my home and has been ever since I was a child."

"So it was you we heard giggling and talking?" he said.

Lumen smiled widely.

"Yes, that was me. I was trying to get you to come through the right path. You wouldn't believe how many people are scared and dart off the path, or go the wrong way. I had to save you somehow; the wolves in this forest are very nasty to travelers."

"How do you stay protected then?" Stanley asked her curiously.

"Willow," said Lumen, looking at him in wonder. "My animal."

"So, you are a Speaker as well?" he asked her, taken back by this new surprise.

"I am — ever since my birth. Willow raised me in this forest. She told me one day I would meet others like myself, and we would go to the city full of people like us, just beyond the Oxen Fields."

Just at that moment, there was a familiar bark from behind them announcing Desmond's return. They turned to see the dog running up the path closest to the hill, Oliver flapping above him. Walking behind them was Elliot, carrying a boar on his back. Casually strolling behind Elliot was the biggest grizzly bear Stanley had ever laid eyes on.

"This," said Lumen, running over to the bear and hugging it around its massive middle, "is Willow Bear."

"Pleased to meet you," said Stanley to the bear, walking over and scratching her head.

"The pleasure is all mine," said Willow. She had a soft voice, but Stanley could sense a strong power in her and knew it would be most unwise to ever anger this bear.

Elliot walked over to them and thudded his hand on Stanley's shoulder.

"Still alive, brother?" he said, grinning over at his friend.

Desmond bounded over and licked Stanley's hand, wagging his tail happily.

"Nice look," he said, looking at the sling on his arm, a rather amused sound to his voice.

"Yes," said Stanley grumbling darkly. "A very fine look."

Willow flopped over and Lumen rubbed her massive belly. They watched her silently. Lumen was one of a kind. She had not witnessed the indecency of men, had not experienced their cruelty. She knew only love for everything; she was a child of nature. Stanley felt a great rush of warmth toward her that he could not explain. He turned to face Elliot.

"I think we may have been wrong about this forest."

"Aye. Was wondering that myself," said Elliot wisely. "But we still shouldn't drop our guard." He whispered to Stanley, "Lumen may not be the only secret of this forest, brother"

"You don't trust her?" he questioned him.

"I trust her fine; it's this forest that I'm worried about," he said quietly.

Desmond, who had been listening to their conversation silently, spoke up.

"We should not linger here long — one night at most. I am sure the lions are still on our trails. We need to get out of the forest and across the fields to the village as fast as we can manage."

So it was settled. The travelers would depart the clearing tomorrow morning. In the meantime, however, they would rest and relax with Lumen. They bathed in the clear pool and washed all of their garments. Later that evening, as the sun began to set and the bugs and insects came out, they settled in Lumen's cave. They lit a fire and roasted the boar they had caught. After their dinner, they sat against the cave wall, smoking their pipes and sending smoke rings out the cave's opening. After a few minutes of watching their majestic and spiraling process, Lumen spoke.

"So you all are leaving in the morning?"

"How did you know that?" Stanley asked her, amazed and full of wonder.

"Sharp ears," she said flatly.

"Well — yes, we are leaving in the morning," Staley replied.

"I'm going to come with you," she said. She had spoken in a way that told them there would be no arguing with her. They simply gaped at her.

"Let me explain it to you," she said with an air of heavy annoyance. "You have no idea how to get out of the forest on your own. This wood is dangerous. And you need my help. I am the only person that can help. I can guide us to the fields where we can continue our road to the village."

After this explanation, they couldn't help agreeing with her. So now four became six, and no one could pretend that they were not very happy about the new change. Elliot pointed out later that having a bear with them would be a big advantage.

"Always a plus," he said with a grin.

The next morning, the company packed all of their belongings and the extra food for the next few days into their packs, slung them over their shoulders, and left on the path.

"I cannot promise that our road will not be dangerous," Lumen said to them as they walked along the path, dew glistening off the leaves and grass as the sun hit the forest. "Lions are numerous in the Oxen Fields, and they will be looking out for you. They may be now waiting for us at the opening; I do now know. We must be on our full guard."

So the company trudged through the new forest path, which was considerably lighter. They didn't need the torches as they did previously. Throughout the day, they saw nothing remotely dangerous or frightening. Stanley was sure it had something to do with Lumen. There was no way the trees would be this revealing and calm if it had been just the original four travelers.

They finally stopped and set up camp by a small stream where several schools of minnows were zooming by every few minutes. The sun had set a few hours ago, so Elliot hastened to get a fire going. He then prepared some water for soup as Oliver went out to hunt. Lumen, Willow, and Desmond were napping peacefully underneath a magnificent pine tree. Stanley was in the woods, foraging for wild mushrooms and herbs to put into the soup.

As he roamed around the trees, he spotted a line of deer wandering through the forest a short way ahead of him. As he walked quietly toward them, he noticed that the line of deer was growing steadily shorter; the deer were simply disappearing from view. His curiosity mounting, he hastened to follow the last deer. As he kept close behind it, he began to see a very wide opening, revealing an enormous grassy field. The deer ahead of him bounded into the grass and disappeared. Stanley reached the opening and saw that the trees were forming yet another arch above him. Stanley had reached the other side of the Deepwood Forest.

The grass was as tall as he was. It was razor sharp and there was no path leading through it. Stanley squinted ahead to try to see beyond the grass waving in the cool night's breeze, but all he could see was more grass, going on forever. He decided to climb up a tree to get a better view. Once he was comfortably situated on a maple tree's largest and sturdiest branch, he gave a gasp of wonder.

As his eyes scanned the field, he saw a dim pinprick of light far off in the distance. Squinting hard, he could make out a large structure surrounding the light, which seemed to be a type of beacon, guiding travelers to its shimmer.

Stanley was looking at the Speakers Village, Arda.

"There's a path ahead of me leading out of the forest!" Stanley yelled to his friends, making them all jump with fright at his commotion as he bumbled noisily back to the campsite.

"Yes, we know," Lumen said calmly to him, still lying on the ground and not opening her eyes.

Stanley stared, bemused at her.

"Well, is there a reason we aren't taking it right now?"

"That's obvious," she said, sounding irritated. "Lions. You saw how tall that grass is. You know full well we wouldn't last an hour out there in the dark on their hunting grounds." She opened an eye and looked at him, smiling. "You really should just relax, Stanley, lie down and stretch your paws." She motioned to the spot next to her.

"Yeah, Stanley," Desmond chimed in as he gave a mighty stretch himself. "Come relax with us."

Elliot came over and handed Lumen and Stanley a cup of tea. He addressed Stanley.

"The soup should be ready for you to add the mushrooms to it now, brother."

Stanley stood silent for a moment. Then with much grumbling, he turned around and headed back up the path. He had left his mushrooms by the field opening.

When he returned, he dropped the mushrooms into the soup and ladled it into wooden bowls for them all. After his dinner, Stanley was feeling less uneasy. Elliot seemed to know that he had something on his mind. He gave him a long deep look for a few minutes. He took out his pipe and sat next to Stanley.

"You all right, brother?" he asked him kindly, drawing on his pipe heavily.

"Yes. I am now," said Stanley looking at Elliot and smiling at his friend.

"Cheers," Lumen's voice came from behind them as she made her way over to sit next to him, wrapping her arms around Elliot and Stanley.

"We will have great adventures together," she said, hugging them tight.

That night, Stanley slept without a care in the world.

Chapter Seven: The Oxen Fields

When Stanley awoke the next morning and opened his eyes, he immediately knew that there was something wrong. Sitting up and staring around, Stanley couldn't see or hear any of his friends. This was most unusual, as Desmond always waited for him to wake, and Elliot usually had a fire going with breakfast cooking.

He strained his ears, listening hard. He thought he heard the howling of a bear in the distance and the barking of a dog. He hastily grabbed his staff with his unbroken arm and ran out of the tent, making his way quickly up the path toward the sounds, now growing louder and more violent as he drew closer. He hoped that his friends were all right and nothing bad had happened to them. As he approached the opening of the forest, he could hear more cries now — cries of humans. Sprinting out of the path into the tall grass, he saw movement to his right.

The second he had entered the grass, he was almost immobile. The grass was so thick and sharp that he could barely take a step a few inches in front of him. As he made his way right, he saw the disturbance. There were now six of the largest lions Stanley had ever seen. They were not alone, however. The lions were now accompanied by two rather evil looking men. One of the men was clad in black armor, a red lion's paw splashed on his chest piece. The second man was wearing a black cloak bearing the same emblem. His was wearing a black tunic, which was ragged and tattered. The man's hands and feet were bound with rope. He looked like he was a prisoner of some kind.

The man clad in armor was clutching a sword and had spotted Stanley. He was now making his way through the grass toward him. Oliver was screeching violently above the lions, swooping down fast and gauging at their eyes with his talons. Several of the lions that had been successfully blinded gave cries and howls of anger and darted off toward the forest. Oliver screeched madly after them, his mighty wings pounding the air. Elliot was in a tussle with a lion, which had darted toward him and leaped into the air at him, bowling him over onto the ground. As he stood up, the lion's paw collided with the side of Elliot's head, knocking him back onto the ground with a thud. He remained still and did not move. As the lion bore down on Elliot, its fangs dripping with drool, there were several twangs from the left. Lumen was firing arrows with such speed and ferocity that Stanley had to duck to avoid getting impaled as an arrow zoomed by him. The arrows flew through the air and made contact with the lion. It dropped to the ground, dead.

The man with the sword was getting closer to Stanley now, but he did not get far. Another twang issued from Lumen's bow and sank into the man's heart, piercing his armor. He stared blankly at them for a second, then thudded to the ground, twitched, and was silent. Willow was taking out a lion close to the woods. Stanley heard clanking and clinking as the man who had been bound was running to the cover of the trees. As quickly as he could, he ran over to Elliot's pack and withdrew his boomerang from it. He was too late. The man met Willow before Stanley could reach him. Willow gave a frightening roar and hit the man across the head with her massive paw. He was out before he hit the ground. Stanley summoned energy from his staff and flung it toward the lions now in the trees. Wind soared toward them and slammed them against the trees with the force of a hurricane. All was silent.

Stanley ran over to Elliot's unconscious body and rolled him over. There was blood running down his face from where he had been struck down by the lion. Stanley shook him violently, but Elliot did not move.

"Elliot!" Stanley yelled, continuing to shake him. "Elliot! Get up!"

Elliot blinked his eyes and groaned, looking around.

"Where'd they go…?" he said wearily to Stanley.

"Gone," he told Elliot, helping him sit up. "We fought them off."

Elliot rubbed his head and wiped the blood off his face. He stood and looked around for his sword. He spotted it lying on the ground a little way ahead. He picked it up and looked around the field. His eyes fell upon the unconscious man lying on the ground a few feet ahead of him, his hands still bound. He walked over slowly to him.

"He's still alive," he said, crouching down and examining the man. He took a length of rope from his bag and tied it to the man's bindings. He then approached Willow.

"May I?" he asked her, holding up the other end of the rope. She nodded, and he tied the other end of the rope around her midsection.

"There," he said brightly smiling at them. "If he wakes up, we can question him without worrying about him escaping. Who would run when they are tied to a bear?"

"Brilliant," said Stanley.

They then ate a very hurried breakfast and began to make their way through the fields, navigating with extreme difficulty in the abysmally tall grass. Elliot took the lead, with Oliver gliding slowly above him. Elliot was slicing at the grass with his sword, making it a little more manageable to walk through. Stanley and Desmond were behind him, and Lumen and Willow made up the rear. Willow dragged the still knocked-out prisoner through the grass behind her. The grass remaining cut into their ankles and the sides of their legs. As Stanley bound his cuts, looking around at the seemingly deserted field, a thought occurred to him.

"Why do they call this place the Oxen Fields?" he asked them at large. "I see no Ox; only Fields."

"Because," said Lumen, sounding sad and morose at this, "long ago, the oxen in this land roamed these beautiful fields and kept them tame as they guarded the village. But when the evil men of the east came with their lions, they slaughtered the oxen, leaving the fields to grow tall and dangerous. They are named the 'Oxen Fields' out of remorse and memory of the magnificent creatures that once roamed here."

Stanley felt a rush of anger toward these unknown men and lions.

"That's awful," he said quietly.

"Evil," muttered Elliot.

As the travelers trudged on through the silent fields, Stanley began to feel uneasy. He couldn't help thinking that more lions were lurking in the grass, waiting. He kept thinking of a lion emerging from the side and taking him down. He clutched his staff tightly and shook the thought from his mind. As they traveled on, their prisoner made no sign of movement or consciousness. He just rolled along on the ground behind Willow; who was careful to make sure to hit the man's head on the hidden rocks and roots buried in the grass as she passed them. The field began to thin out now, the grass getting less brutal; a few trees had begun to come into vision on the horizon ahead of them. They had reached the edge of the plains.

They set up camp just before nightfall. They tied their immobile prisoner against a tree and started a fire. They cooked their last scraps of meat, their spirits high despite their lack of food. They would reach the village tomorrow morning, their journey was nearly complete. A short way ahead of their camp was a path flanked by large spruce trees that headed down a hill and out of sight. This path was the most direct way to the Speakers Village. Arda was ahead. Stanley was thoroughly excited at this news. For one thing, his body was sorer than it had ever been in his life. Secondly, he was excited to learn and meet other Speakers, and have all the time in the world to learn the ways of the Speaker. There was no energy left in his body. He felt his eyes getting heavy and his head drooping.

A few hours later, Stanley jumped awake. His back was propped against a tree, and his head seemed to have rolled onto his shoulder. He stood up and gave a great stretch, looking around as he did. Desmond was sleeping at his feet, curled up in a ball. He was curled up next to Willow, a small smile on his face, his tongue lolling out. Elliot and Lumen were sleeping peacefully in the tent. Oliver was awake and perched on a tree, staring down at Stanley, his head cocked to its side.

The man they had caught earlier that day was now awake. It took Stanley a few minutes to realize this, and when he did realize it, he also noticed that the man was staring directly at him. Stanley made his way over to the strange man, noticing how the man's eyes followed his every movement.

"How long have you been awake, then?" he asked the man staring up at him.

The man did not answer him. He only looked up at Stanley with large, bulbous blue eyes. His eyes seemed to emanate a piercing feeling, as though Stanley was being read by his movements. The man looked intellectual and had a very weary and sickly look about him. They had found no weapon on him when they searched him.

"What is your name?" Stanley tried.

"Robert," said the man slowly, still not taking his eyes off Stanley.

The man spoke in almost a whisper; his voice was so quiet Stanley had to lean in to hear him speak.

"All right then, Robert," said Stanley, crouching down. "Let's talk about what to do with you."

Without warning, Robert kicked Stanley hard in the face. Stanley fell backwards onto the ground, clutching his nose, blood now seeping through his fingers. Desmond jumped up from his sleeping place and darted toward Robert, his teeth bared. At the same time, Oliver gave a loud screech and zoomed down from his perch at Robert. Desmond bit into Robert's arm, and Oliver was pecking madly as he soared above Robert's head. Robert screamed in agony; he could not defend himself, as he was still tied to the tree. Lumen came running out of the tent, followed closely by Elliot. Willow sat up sleepily at all of the commotion as well, but she did not move otherwise. Stanley stood up, his eyes watering, wiping the blood from his nose with his good arm. The two animals stopped their attack on Robert as the others came running toward them, leaving Robert whimpering, covered in scratches and minor bite-marks.

"Oh my goodness, Stanley, what happened?" asked Lumen, running over to him. "Are you all right?"

"I'm fine," said Stanley angrily. Then gesturing toward Robert, he said, "But he's about to not be."

Elliot walked over to Robert, his sword in his hand. Robert looked terrified.

"Please don't kill me!" he shrieked.

"Excuse me, brother?" said Elliot darkly to him. "Remember that your mates tried to do us in today; it's no more than you deserve."

"No," said Robert quickly. "I was about to be murdered by the same group that attacked you. You just walked up at the wrong time."

Desmond, who was now sitting by Stanley's feet, laughed.

"And I suppose you think we forgot about the lions tailing us. Explain that one."

"Easy," said Robert simply, looking over at the dog. "Those lions were hunting; they cared nothing of your pitiful journey. However, the lion leading the pack was mine."

"Oh really?" said Elliot, now smiling at Robert, still gripping his sword tightly. "I hope you know I put it out of its misery for you, brother."

"Yes. I know this," said Robert, turning his head to stare at Elliot with his piercing eyes. "That was why I was being executed. You see, where I'm from, when you lose your animal, your life is taken."

Elliot looked downcast at this news. He turned around without a word and went back into the tent. Oliver returned to his perch and stared at Robert menacingly, as though daring him to move. Lumen ran into the tent to comfort Elliot, giving Stanley a tight hug before doing so. Stanley and Desmond remained standing rooted to the spot, looking at Elliot. Robert simply stared at Stanley. After a few moments more of silence, Stanley and Desmond retreated to the tent. Before he entered it, he turned to Robert.

"I'm Stanley."

Robert said nothing.

The next morning, all of the travelers awoke at the same time. They got a fire going and had a long talk about what to do with Robert. In the end, it was decided by Elliot that they would unbind the man and let him go with them to the village, and then he was free to do what he wished.

"I really don't think he's a threat anymore," Elliot told them all around the fire. "He's got no means of defense."

So they unbound Robert and told him the plan they had for him. Robert smiled brightly at them as they undid him from the tree. He stood up and hugged them all in turn. He then cooked a fat load of sausages for them all. Soon enough, their bellies were feeling comfortably full. It was time for the last bit of their trek. With high hopes, the travelers packed up their camp and belongings and before long were prepared to set off. Elliot had instructed Robert to carry all of the water packs. Lumen walked over to him, Willow by her side.

"I'm sorry about last night," she said warmly to the Robert, who was struggling with the heavy jugs.

Robert grinned.

"Thank you all for saving my life," he said to all of the travelers, a tear running down his face.

They all smiled at him.

"No problem," said Stanley and Desmond together.

The path toward the village was absolutely beautiful. The sky was a deep blue and the sun was shining brightly above them. The path led down a hill, flanked with trees. At the bottom of the hill was the greenest grass they had ever seen. It seemed to dance instead of wave as the wind blew through it. Looking straight ahead, they saw the village. Standing tall against the horizon was a large wooden fence that seemed to stretch on in either direction for miles and miles. Behind it, posted off far in the distance, there was what looked like a watchtower. As they drew nearer to the village, the voices grew louder. They were coming up on the entrance of the village. Standing by a large iron gate was a gallant looking guard, with a hippo by his side. When the guard spotted the travelers, he stood up straighter, and hailed them majestically.

"Greetings, Speakers. It is with good grace that I welcome you to Arda."

Chapter Eight: The Speakers Village

"Open the gates!" the man yelled to a group of men perched atop the wall of the city.

The men began to pull on a massive rope, and the gates began to slowly creep open. Lumen gasped. Elliot said "Blimey." Stanley stared, transfixed at what he was seeing.

They were looking at a beautiful cobbled street, winding around the building and shops, splitting off into new roads. Some of the shops were built from wood, others from marble. A sign hung above them reading:

Welcome To Arda

Population As Follows

Non-Speakers — 4,000

Speakers — 8,000

Animals — 9,000

Stanley stared in wonder at the shops and streets around them. There were people and animals alike bustling through the street, popping in and out of the various shops and buildings. There was a fat bald man sitting behind a small vendor's tent of what seemed to be maggots and other insects. There was a ferret sitting on his shoulder, waving at the various people passing by. A man walking a short way ahead of them had hundreds of vivid green snakes wriggling around his arms, hissing slightly as he whispered to them. There was a very old man with a cane walking next to them, a sloth moving comfortably slow by his side. A majestic white tiger was curled up on a rug in a window of a shop that read: Tiger Jewels — Stones and gems for all occasions.

A short way ahead, there was a wizened old woman behind a stand, with an armadillo sitting on the countertop, smiling at the passerby. A sign hung above her tent reading: Remedy Plants and More — Everyday remedies for everyday problems.

An assortment of herbs, flowers, and oils was spread out in

various bowls on the countertop.

As they walked up the long winding street, Stanley stared around in wonder. He spotted a rather large sign ahead of them. As they reached it, they saw the sign was inscribed with various names. Arrows were pointing off in the direction of the streets. It read as follows:

Town Hall — Straight
Town Square — Straight
Speaker Housing — Left
Non-Speaker Housing — Right
Shamans Hall — Diagonal Right
Lookout Tower — Diagonal Left
Animal House Pub — Left
Shops and Monument — Straight
Potioneer, Defensive HQ, Guardsmen Housing — Right

Stanley looked at his friends excitedly.

"What should we do first?" he asked them curiously.

It was Elliot who spoke first.

"Let's have a sit down in the pub and have a drink. We have had a very long journey."

So the travelers took a left, and headed down a more narrow, dark, dingy, and dirty street. They passed more people and animals as they strolled along, but the atmosphere on this street was not merry and jolly as the main road had been. Many of the people had nasty, evil looks about them. They had the obvious looks of thieves and plunderers. There was a very thin man with a wispy mustache whispering to a small fat badger on his porch. They passed an alley where a man was surrounded by at least thirty crows. He was cowered against the wall, trembling as the birds advanced on him. As they hurried past, they heard the man give out a scream. A short way ahead, they saw a very old wooden sign sticking out from a very dirty looking building.

Animal House Pub
Owner: Arland Whistleworthy
Friendly To All Peoples And Animals
Locations In Arda And Elda

Due To Space And Capacity Issues, We Ask That Any Animal Larger Than A Dog Is To Remain Outside.

Thank You,

Management

Robert said that he would meet them in a few minutes, and walked up the street, his tattered cloak billowing. Lumen said she would be inside once she convinced Willow to sit outside. So Elliot pushed open the pub's heavy, creaky door. As they entered, they looked at Willow, who looked dejected.

The inside of the pub was small, shabby, and grimy. Smoke hung thick in the air like fog, and the smell was somewhat foul. They could smell the decades of animals and people coming and going. They approached the bar.

The barman was a rather small and weedy looking man, with tangled gray hair that stuck out in all directions. He had small, watery gray eyes and a very unfriendly look about him. He was handing a glass to a man who was having an animated conversation with a fox. The barman turned and greeted them.

"Hello there, lads," he squeaked at them in a tiny voice, which took them by surprise. Stanley had been expecting a grunt. "What can I get fer ya?"

"Hello there, brother," said Elliot jovially. "I think we'll take two flagons of mead and some water for our companions."

"Right you are, then," said the barman, and he sidled off behind a door that led to the kitchen and cellars to fetch their drinks.

As they waited for him to return, Stanley looked around in fascination, taking in the pub and all of its inhabitants. There was a group of soldiers clad in silver armor and acid green cloaks, who were all sitting together at a corner table. They were huddled together and talking in hushed voices. A group of bobcats clad in the same silver armor sat next to them, listening to their every word. A woman at a table to their left was stroking a large iguana and sipping on cup of tea that was steaming slightly. A waiter was bumbling around the pub, passing out drinks that were being held up in midair by four finches.

Lumen entered the pub and made her way around it to where they sat, just as the barman was returning with their drinks. The barman saw Lumen and simply gaped at her odd appearance.

"I'll take a steaming wine, please," she said, smiling at the tiny barman.

The barman grumbled and sidled off once more, and Lumen turned to face them.

"This place is very interesting, isn't it?" she said, excitement ringing in her voice.

"Aye," said Elliot, staring around as he sipped happily on his drink.

The barman returned, carrying a steaming glass of red wine for Lumen. The pub door creaked open and in came Robert carrying a loaf of bread. Stanley took notice that Robert had disposed of his cloak. Robert spotted them and walked over and sat down with them.

"A glass of your best ale, please," he said to the barman.

The barman, looking very grumpy now, sidled off, grumbling about his workload. Robert stared at all of them. He looked very nervous, as if he needed to get something out.

"What's up?" Stanley asked him curiously. "What is on your mind?"

"Well," said Robert, looking more uncomfortable now, "I know that I am free to go on my own and do as I wish, but it is not what I wish. I wish to stay with you. If that's all right . . ." He said all of this very fast.

Stanley smiled at him and looked at his friends; all of them were beaming at Robert as well.

"The more the merrier," said Elliot in a jolly voice.

The barman returned, now carrying a tall glass of dark brown ale for Robert.

"You lot new?" he inquired of them, handing Robert his drink.

"Aye," said Elliot burping.

"Well then," he squeaked, "you'll wanna go to town hall and let them know you are new. They will give you proper housing." He eyed Elliot for a moment before speaking once more.

"It would be a good idea for you to go down to the guardsmen and volunteer for scouting, my lad. They need all the help they can get, especially in these times," the barman said to Elliot.

"Why would it be a good idea?" said Elliot, who looked doubtful.

"And what do you mean 'these times'?"

The barman sighed deeply and refilled their glasses for them. The barman then snapped his fingers, and a chimpanzee emerged from the kitchen, wearing a chef's jacket. The chimp made his way to the barman and spoke to him in a low voice.

"What can I do for you, sir?" he asked gruffly.

"I need you to watch the bar for the moment while I inform our new guests of the town's trouble," the barman said kindly to his chimp.

"Right you are, sir," it grunted. The chimp then began to place more drinks on the waiter's tray, as the finches fluttered around him, chirping out new drink orders.

The barman pulled up a chair and faced them.

"The lions and the Blackfoots are getting restless," he said sadly. "We need all the help we can get to keep this town safe."

"We know about the lions," said Stanley hurriedly. "But who are these Blackfoots you speak of?"

"They are a group of Speakers, nearly as old as the Eldans themselves," he said, sighing again before continuing. "They are cruel and wicked and they follow an evil man whose madness is growing. It is he who founded them. They gain what they need by carrying out his orders. They have been silent for some time now, but recently, they have emerged again. They have begun to waylay travelers, stealing their supplies and killing them if they fight back. It is a very terrible thing."

"That's awful," said Lumen in a scared voice. Her hand was covering her mouth in shock.

"Aye," squeaked the tiny old barman. "They live northwest of the village, in the Blackhill Rock, a massive rock quarry that goes on for miles and miles. It has been rumored that their numbers have increased in the past few years.'

Stanley looked over at Robert, who was shifting slightly in his seat.

The barman stood up.

"You lot be careful now," he said as he scuttled off, returning to his busy bar.

They all looked at one another, their minds racing.

"Well," said Elliot, finishing his drink in a gulp and standing up. "I guess we should have a look at the rest of the town, then."

They all finished their drinks hastily and exited the dim pub. The sun was shining brightly above them as they entered the dirty street. Stanley looked at the building around him. He spotted a small koala bear staring at him from a window a few floors above him. He ignored it and followed his friends up the road to the main street. The cobbled street was empty now; most of the occupants were inside the elegant looking buildings or otherwise performing their jobs. There were a few vendors posted outside, and they smiled at them as they walked by. Elliot found it highly amusing when a group of giggling mice attempted to steal several apples before being chased away by a small gray tabby cat.

Stanley stared around, his heart racing with excitement. He had finally made it! It was like wandering in a dream. He smiled broadly as they passed a man and his monkey, both holding their brooms and sweeping the cobbled street in perfect unison. Elliot gave a gasp of wonder and turned to look ahead. They had reached the town square.

The town square was circular shaped, with elegant tents around its edges, all unoccupied at the moment. The vendors in these tents would only be around once a week. These were the traveling traders. They wandered the world finding artifacts, weapons, and in some cases stray animals to bring back to Arda for purchase or trade. Set in the middle of the town square was a massive fountain, a shimmering pool gleaming around the life-size statues of a man and a dog. As they drew closer, the features on the statue became more distinguishable.

The man was strong and noble looking. He wore long robes and held a sword up in one hand; in the other was a great staff of oak. His facial structure was strikingly similar to Stanley. The man had Stanley's crooked nose and his curly hair. The dog was unmistakable. It was Desmond.

"It there a reason you didn't tell us there's a monument for your dog here, brother?" Elliot asked him, sounding surprised.

"I had no idea myself," he said, sounding just as surprised as Elliot.

They both looked at Desmond. Lumen, however, spoke first.

"There's a plaque here, look," she said, pointing to a large golden

W. F. Mick

plaque that was set at the bottom of the statue.

> This monument is dedicated to Simon Goodguard and his dog Desmond.
> The Founders of Arda.
>
> Simon fell fighting bravely during the attack led by Hart Blackfoot. Desmond led Simon's wife and unborn child to safety. His whereabouts are currently unknown. Simon came from Elda, carrying The Book of Teachings with him to this location. He founded the land of Arda, the community of people and animals alike.
>
> *All Proceeds Go to the Shamans Hall for Research*

It was Desmond who spoke first. He turned to face Stanley, his head bowed low in apology.

"I'm sorry I didn't tell you," he said. "It was something you needed to find out for yourself."

"It's quite all right," said Stanley smiling, and patting Desmond on the back.

Desmond wagged his tail happily.

"Well," said Elliot rather awkwardly, "I think I will go sign us in at the town hall and get accommodations."

"I think I will come with you," said Robert next to him.

They wandered off to the right, in the direction of the town hall.

Lumen muttered about going to the herbalist and potioneers and wandered off, humming happily to herself, Willow strolling casually by her side. Stanley stared at the statue in front of him.

"So this man . . ." he said to Desmond thoughtfully, "this man is my father, isn't he?"

"Yes," said Desmond slowly.

"Good looking fellow," said Stanley, smiling at Desmond.

"He was a shaman, too, you know," said Desmond insightfully. "He started this village with your mother and another Speaker years and years ago. The other Speaker was Hart Blackfoot. On the way to this place, Simon stumbled upon a small puppy drowning in a swamp. He rescued me and I revealed myself to him. We sailed from Elda to Varia. We landed on a coast and met another Speaker: Hart."

Desmond sighed deeply, also looking at the statue.

"At first, all was well. But over time, Hart grew jealous inside; he grew jealous of your father's gifts. When Simon met your mother, Mindy, they all traveled here and started this great community. But it did not remain great for long."

"What happened?" asked Stanley, eager to hear more.

"Hart became too soaked in the greed and strength of his powers. He began to grow evil inside. He recruited evil men to steal and plunder in the name of Arda. He killed those who opposed him, mainly the non-Speakers. He called them impure and imperfect beings, incapable of ever understanding our ways. He believed that non-Speakers did not belong here."

"Why didn't my father or the rest of the village do anything?" asked Stanley, amazed at this news.

"We knew nothing about it until it was too late," said Desmond sorrowfully. "When your father discovered his treachery, he banned him from this land forever, but before he left, Hart and his followers attacked the village and attempted to steal *The Book of Teachings*. They failed to steal the book, but they murdered a fair amount of the people here — Speakers and non-Speakers alike. Your father was among them."

"What is *The Book of Teachings*?" he asked his dog.

But Desmond did not get to answer, for a very old man had approached them as they talked. He was wearing green robes, with a bag of plants hanging at his side, and he was holding a very knobby staff. The man had a thin little beard, no hair, and twinkling green eyes.

"Desmond?" he said to the dog, a look of surprised amazement on his wrinkly old face.

Desmond wagged his tail, and bounded over to him, allowing the man to scratch his head. The old man then looked over at Stanley. For a few moments, the man gaped at him, taking in every inch of his appearance. The man must have realized what he was doing for he gave a small shake of his head and addressed Stanley.

"Forgive me for staring, my dear boy, but you look ever so

much like your father," said the old man squeakily.

Stanley didn't know what to say or how to react to this comment, so he just remained silent.

"What is your name, my boy?" inquired the wizened shaman.

"Stanley," he replied.

"Well, Stanley," said the old man, "if you would, please follow me."

Stanley did not move. He did not know if he wanted to go with this man anywhere.

"Follow you where?" Stanley asked him curiously.

"To the Shamans' Hall," said the man simply, as if anyone could've guessed this. "I'm taking you to your quarters: the chamber where your father stayed long ago, my lad."

Excitement flooded Stanley at these words. The old man grabbed him by the arm and led him to a side street. As they walked, the street wound around and about. At the end of the street was a large iron gate. Behind the gate sat a massive building made of white marble. It had four floors and thick heavy wooden doors. Above the massive wooden doors were etched the words Shamans' Hall. A gold plaque hanging on a post to the right of the doors read:

> *To all followers, this building is dedicated to the shamans of the earth. The people of the earth who study the book of teachings brought from Elda by Simon Goodguard. He gave his life defending the lands about. We continue his teachings and his legacy here forevermore.*
>
> **Arda Shaman Society**

The old man pushed the heavy doors open with a grunt, and Stanley's mouth fell open. He was looking upon a great study hall, but it was unlike anything he had seen before. The entire floor was wooded. Trees stood tall, all the way to the massive ceiling. The earthy floor was covered with thick moss, like a furry green carpet. Bookshelves full of volumes were placed precariously all around the trees throughout the hall. As Stanley followed the old man (who was heading toward a door in the back of the hall), he noticed the eyes of the other shamans staring at him, or bending over to their fellows to whisper something excitedly to them. It made him feel very uncomfortable.

The old man had reached the wooden door in the back of the hall and pushed it open. He waited for Stanley to reach him, smiling at him as he made his way forward into a large room with a massive iron staircase that wound up toward the other floors. They made their way up the staircase, peeking into the other rooms as they went.

The second floor of the hall was devoted to plant life: flowers of the most vivid hues of blue, red, and purple shining in the dim light of the room. The third floor was devoted to the arts of divination, mind training, and elemental control. The room was full of tables holding crystal balls, shimmering swirls of smoke rippling inside them. Some shamans were staring inside the depths of the crystal, completely focused, trying to see within. When they reached the fourth landing, the old man pushed open the door.

They were now in a very large but comfortable-looking room. There was a beautiful four-poster bed placed at the back of the room. Chairs and hassocks were scattered about the room, circling a glass case near the fireplace, which was set in the right corner, by a window.

"This is where your mother and father lived, my dear boy," said the old man, his eyes twinkling in the light. "It is all yours now, Stanley."

Smiling, he departed the room, closing the door softly behind him, leaving Stanley and Desmond alone. Desmond gave a stretch and a yawn and flopped over onto a hassock, relaxed and tired. Stanley, however, made his way to the glass case. Drawing close to it, he saw that there was a very old and very tattered leather book inside of it. He removed the glass and picked up the fragile looking book. It was very dusty; the dust covered the words inscribed into the book's cover. He blew away the dust, coughing and sneezing as he did so. He could now read the words on the cover:

The Book of Teachings
Here in these pages are the teachings of the Speakers of Elda.
Read with good grace and pass the knowledge on forevermore.

As Stanley opened the book, a parchment envelope fell out of it onto the ground. Stanley leaned down and picked it up, and he saw with surprise that it was addressed to him. Thick letters were splashed across its front reading:

To My Son,

Stanley

Stanley hastily opened the letter, adrenaline pumping through his veins as he pulled a slip of parchment from the envelope. He sat down in a chair, unfolded the paper, and began to read the letter.

To my son,

When you read this, know that it was me that has chosen your path. You have been blessed with a great gift and power ever since you were born. Trust in Desmond; he will guard you and guide you. Trust in him above all others. Next, I wish you to use this book to promote the ways and lasting ideals of our people, as I fear it may wander away from their minds. The world is turning to greed and evil; you must not let this happen. For if it does, peril will meet us all. I hope you and your mother make it safely back to Arda one day. Never falter from being the person that you are. Never accept the fact that power and greed are better than peace and prosperity. My good grace follows you forevermore in life. I will always be in your heart and mind.

With Love,
Simon.

Tears were falling silently down Stanley's face, and he was trembling slightly. He fondled the book now in his hands and stood up, wiping his eyes and sniffing. He threw off his pack and baggage, staring around the comfy room. He walked over to Desmond, who was now curled up in a ball, sleeping placidly next to the window. Stanley stared out the window, looking down at his father's statue.

He smiled broadly to himself.

"We are home, Desmond."

Chapter Nine: The Book of Teachings

The news traveled quickly that the founder's heir was now living in the village, so that over the next few weeks, Stanley found himself being followed everywhere he went. People and animals alike would surround him within minutes of leaving a building, all chattering madly and recommending suggestions for him. This annoyed Stanley very much, but he had a very easy solution to this problem. He would simply spot one of his friends and proceed to talk to them, and eventually, after being ignored for a minute or two, the crowd would disperse, thoroughly downcast. Lumen was especially good at this, as the crowd never got too close to Willow. It is very unwise to crowd a bear. Many people on the grimy side streets of the village would go out of their way to get a glimpse of him as well, always craning their necks or doing double takes as he passed them. Most of the looks he was given were far from excited and respectful. They were unpleasant leers and taunting smiles, as if they knew something that Stanley did not. It made him feel very uncomfortable and uneasy.

The friends spent most of their time throughout the next few weeks exploring the many treasures the village had to offer. There was Paws and Claws, a spa for the animals of Arda to enjoy. There was a multitude of food vendors that sold delicacies from all over the world of Varia. Once a week, there was a conference in the town's amphitheater, which was located on the outer wall of the village. Many traveling vendors were also popping in and out of Arda, so you never knew what would be available day by day. The Shamans' Hall offered classes on becoming one with your animal counterparts and various healing remedies for when you are in the wild. The best part of it all was that Stanley fit in.

They were all very busy now that they had settled in a little, but the friends met each night in the Animal House Pub to relax together and talk about their days. Elliot and Oliver had joined the Arda Guardsmen and had been responsible for the capture of at least thirty Blackfoot members in the past week. These captures were looked at as a great advancement on the village's efforts against Hart and his men. The village was treating Elliot with the same esteem that Stanley was receiving. Elliot, however, said that the captures made him feel guilty.

"None of these men had animals, and what's more, they barely put up a fight. Most of 'em willingly surrendered to us. I feel bad because they were no threat. It is all very confusing."

Lumen had begun an apprenticeship at Honeybee Potions where she would learn complex potions for a multitude of scenarios and situations from Arda's master potioneer, Wilbert Brewst. Wilbert Brewst had come from Elda and had in fact sailed over on the same ship that bore Desmond and Simon and was part of the group of Speakers that had originally settled Arda.

Many of the villagers (men mostly) would turn their heads in wonder and awe as Lumen passed. She was disliked by nearly all of the women for this and was given very dark and judgmental looks from them. Some of the villagers would often laugh openly at her clothes. Stanley had to remind himself that although he was used to Lumen's eccentric appearance, most of the villagers were not accustomed to seeing someone who was dressed in leaves. Most of the town, however, loved her and found her equal love for everything inspiring.

Robert, however, was a different story. Since Robert had no animal, he was currently living on one of the grimy side streets, in the non-Speakers housing. These were smaller and simpler than the Speaker houses, which varied in size depending on the animal being accommodated. Most of the villagers would spit in the road as he walked by and people coming from the opposite direction would go out of their way to bump into him, often knocking him off his feet. Whenever Stanley would attempt to tell these people off for being so intolerant, Robert would stop him and simply say it was because he was without an animal and all of his friends have them.

"Many people believe I'm faking," he told Stanley solemnly on day as they walked through the streets of the village. "Many think I am not a Speaker, which I am merely pretending to be. Just ignore them as I do."

Stanley wasn't quite sure about this explanation. The other

non-Speakers got along very well with the Speakers in Arda, and none of them were treated like Robert. But Stanley obeyed his friend's wishes and ignored these occurrences. Even the animals showed some animosity toward him. Stanley and Robert would go out during the days Stanley wasn't devoted to his studies and look at the many animals that the travelers would bring from all over the lands. They searched all day for an animal for Robert but without any luck. None seemed to want anything to do with him. The animals would turn their backs to him, revealing their backsides. There was one nasty incident one day with a monkey. The monkey had attempted to throw its dung at him, but Robert had ducked, resulting in the dung hitting a rhinoceros straight in his face. Robert had to endure fifteen minutes of death threats from the dung-splattered creature, all the while insisting that it was the monkey. He ended up having to pay the stand owner some gold for causing the uproar and was very grumpy the rest of the day.

When Stanley and Desmond were not with their friends, they could be found in the Shamans' Hall for Stanley was taking various lessons to expand his studies. First, he would start the day by reading lore books in the lower chamber. He would read until lunch time. He then would go out for a bite. After lunch, he was back inside the hall for herb lore. He would learn to care for various types of plant life that were found all over Arda. He would learn every property the plant had to offer and then take the plants and herbs that were dry and mash them into various medicine powders and potions, often having to work late into the day, sweating in the hot greenhouse as he pored over instructional books and scrolls. This lesson took up the rest of his day, and he was not free again until supper.

When he returned, he had a small lesson with the other shamans on elemental control. The shamans would gather together and hone their skills by dueling with each other. When they were finished with this, they all sat and meditated together before retreating to their homes. Stanley would go upstairs to his quarters and talk with Desmond about the day's lessons, or he and his companion would stroll the lamp-lit streets, enjoying the calm and serenity, sometimes running into another late night wanderer and having a short chat.

Stanley also spent a great amount of his time reading *The*

Book of Teachings. Robert was to be found with him whenever he did this, as he had become fascinated by the book. It was Speaker legend, one of the oldest forms of history. He would read excitedly over Stanley's shoulder and often ask to borrow the book so that he could read it at his leisure.

So one chilly autumn day, a few months after they had come to Arda, Stanley, Desmond, and Robert could be found in Stanley's quarters, poring over the book. The book was open to a chapter entitled: Elemental Control: A Short Introduction.

> The world around you holds energy of a magnificent kind. It is called Elemental Energy, and it is the energy released by all living things. Out of all beings, humans are the only ones who can control and harness this great wonder. The energy can be used to heal, to defend oneself, or even to protect oneself. It is used most commonly by shamans. If put into the wrong hands, Elemental Control can be dangerous. This is a practice known as *The Forbidden Teachings*. This form of Elemental Control is to be studied but never practiced. Through the course of time and lessons, the individual will become more familiar with the elements and therefore more capable of using them when needed.
>
> Below are the various forms of Elemental Control followed by a brief description. (More information can be found with further study and reading.)
>
> Forms of Elemental Control
>
> Water Control: Ability to manipulate water and its various forms (i.e., Ice, Liquid, and Gas)
>
> Fire Control: Ability to manipulate fire (Fire cannot be created, only bended.)
>
> Earth Control: Ability to manipulate the forms of earth (i.e., Plant life, rock, various small life forms, such as insects)
>
> Wind Control: Ability to manipulate winds
>
> The Forbidden Teachings: The ability to manipulate the mind (*never practiced*). The ability to manipulate Dark Mass (*never practiced*)
>
> Ways of using elemental control vary from subject to subject.
>
> Some can bend elements with their minds, though this takes nearly a lifetime of practice and concentration to learn. Some use their hands, but this is as just as difficult as mind manipulation.
>
> Elements are most harnessed by the use of a staff. Bamboo is highly efficient, as well as holly, oak, maple, dogwood, ash, and willow.

> Some shamans, (and in some instances, scouts and warriors) have been known to use their hands for Elemental Control. This can come in extremely handy when dealing with —

Stanley looked up; he was starting to feel tired. He stood up and stretched, looking over at Robert whose eyes were still glued in the book's depths.

"Want to go out for a bit, try to find an animal for you?" he asked his friend, failing to stifle a yawn.

Robert jumped and looked at him. Stanley thought Robert's eyes looked oddly strained, and he was almost certain that it had nothing to do with the reading.

"What?" he asked Stanley in a distant, almost hollow voice.

"Let's go find you an animal. I think today might be your lucky day," said Stanley, looking down at his friend with some concern. "Come on, you look tired; a little sun will do you good."

Robert hesitated, his eyes returning to the book.

"I don't know," he said warily, not looking at Stanley. "What's the point? There is no animal that wants to have me as a companion. I've failed."

"No you haven't," replied Stanley genially, laughing a little at this comment. "You just need to find the right fit. Now, get up and come with me."

Robert stood up, smiling as he did so, and the two excited men left the hall into the breezy autumn afternoon, Desmond trotting along casually beside them. They made their way up the beautiful cobbled streets, winding this way and that, until they reached the view of the monument of Stanley's father. The mixed sounds of many animals and people met their ears as they approached the square. The tents were bursting to the brim with animals today, all of them screeching, barking, hissing, and spitting. Signs were hanging in front of the various tents, and they read them as they looked inside. A tent saying Exotics was carrying a multitude of very beautiful animals, including a stunningly white tiger that was pacing its cage menacingly, as if daring someone to come closer. Other signs read things like: Common Woodland Animals, Ice Type/Polar Area, Snakes and Lizards Galore (All Types), Marsh Dwellers, Sea Types, Birds and Beasts, and a very rough and ragged tent held a decaying sign that read: Unmanageable.

This last tent caught their eyes in particular. A very small and fat bushy haired man with a beard to match was attempting to control his uncontrollable animals. A large honey badger was darting back and forth in his cage, rattling the bars madly as he did so, which was irritating all of the other animals. There was a moose howling as if it were a wolf, drooling slightly. As they approached, the moose banged his head furiously against his cage, making an attempt to maim them. A large cage held thirty mad gray squirrels that were all scuttling around their makeshift habitat of branches, so that they looked like small gray blurs, darting back and forth. How this man had managed to find, capture, and travel with these animals to Arda was a mystery to them. The owner of the tent was attempting to wrestle a particularly large kangaroo back into its cage, which it seemed to have broken out of. A sign above the cage read: "Charlie — Hill-Land fighting kangaroo. Caution: High energy animal, only those who travel or roam abroad can buy. Should not be put into small house or confined area. Purchase at own risk."

The man gave a groan and fell to the ground, clutching at his gut. The kangaroo had kicked him hard with such force that he was propelled across the tent, slamming the ground hard. The kangaroo proceeded to hop over to Robert, who had been watching the man's struggles with an amused expression on his face. Robert's hilarity changed to horror as the animal approached him, however, its speed gaining. Desmond had begun barking at it as it neared. Ignoring him, the kangaroo jumped right over him with ease, and landed in front of Robert. For a few minutes, they simply stared at each other, the kangaroo bouncing slightly on the balls of its massive feet.

"Yes?" Robert asked it cautiously, his voice ringing with nervousness, and his body trembling.

The kangaroo punched him directly in the nose, and then kicked him hard into a cart of fruit a short way away. As he got up, Robert was clutching his stomach in one hand, and his now bleeding nose in the other. He looked up at the kangaroo, who had hopped over to him in one mighty leap. The kangaroo smacked him in the gut with his tail, sending him flying backwards again, this time slipping on the fruit strewn about the ground from the wreckage of the cart. He looked rough. Stanley thought his nose might be broken, and his eye was starting to blacken from where

Charlie had hit him.

"What on earth did you do that for?" he bellowed furiously at the beast, his voice ringing in the now silent square. Almost all eyes were on Robert now. "What have I done to deserve this?"

The kangaroo simply bounced up and down excitedly, evidently thrilled Robert was speaking to it.

"I'm choosing you," it said to him, ceasing its hopping and picking Robert up off the ground in one motion. The kangaroo towered above him. Robert was staring up at it now with some interest, a hand still clutching his bloody nose.

"Me?" he gaped, looking fascinated by this request. "You want me as a companion?"

"Yes," said Charlie heartily to him, resuming his mad hopping.

Stanley and Desmond had begun to laugh as they watched Robert pay for Charlie, handing the much relived tent owner a large sack of gold with a very unsatisfied and sour look on his face. The rest of the afternoon was spent watching Charlie beat up Robert in a loving way. As they walked around, Charlie would occasionally hit Robert upside the back of his head with his palms or otherwise trip him up with his tail. Stanley knew that Robert was doing all he could manage to not lose his temper with Charlie. He knew Robert was very happy inside to have a companion now, and Charlie had been locked in that cage for a very long time.

"He just needs some exercise," he would say to them, getting to his feet with Stanley's help for the eighth time that afternoon, after being dropkicked by Charlie. "The upside is that I will get better accommodations now, although I'm sure I'll be paying for damages quite often. I'm sure he will break things." He sighed heavily at this comment, though, sounding vaguely agitated.

The next night, Robert and Stanley, joined by Desmond and Charlie, were in the Shamans' Hall, once again reading *The Book of Teachings*. The book was open to a section entitled Dark Mass.

> **Dark** mass is created when one uses Elemental Control to perform acts of evil. It is known to dwell in mountains, hidden deep in their chasms. If left unchecked for an extended period of time, it can burst. This burst will destroy anything in its path, depending on the mass size and stamina. Many Dark Speakers

who dwell in the caves and mountains and practice the forbidden teachings use it for their evil notions. Dark Mass can be altered from its damaging form, but only by those who are pure of heart, that is to say, those who love. When touched by loving hands, the mass is altered to a beautiful shimmering light that bursts into energy for all life to use for many years.

Under these words were several illustrations. A group of rather evil looking men were holding a ball of purplish smoke, grinning manically. Another image depicted a rather noble looking man releasing a golden light into the sky. Desmond, who was lying by their feet curled up and napping most peacefully, gave a mighty stretch and stood up to look at Stanley.

"This is why Hart Blackfoot wants *The Book of Teachings*," he said to them sharply.

They looked at him inquiringly at this new scrap of information.

"What do you mean?" asked Stanley in wonder.

"Hart is obsessed with the Forbidden Teachings and Dark Mass. He has always been this way, even since the beginning, although he was much better at concealing it back then. He is always searching for more knowledge on it, for he knows very little about it, or at least he did when we last met. He would beg your father for information, but your father saw through him and revealed nothing to him."

The friends stared blankly at Desmond. Desmond sighed at their silence, sounding irritated, and continued on.

"He wants this book," he said, gesturing at the book with his nose. "He wants to learn all he can about Dark Mass. His goal is to wipe out this village and all of its inhabitants."

"But — but why?" Stanley stammered. "Why would any person want that?"

"Because without the constant and vigilant resistance from this village, Hart would be free to enslave the lands surrounding us — and if any resist, they will meet their doom."

A loud thud issued from their, left making them jump with fright and look over at Robert. Charlie had just hit him in the back of his head, causing him to hit his face on the table rather hard. Stanley looked back to Desmond.

"But — but surely there isn't any Dark Mass near Arda," he said to his dog in a worried voice.

Desmond sighed.

"Unfortunately, yes," he replied gravely. "The only known form of Dark Mass in these lands lies deep in the mountains northeast of here. When he was exiled, Hart and his men came upon it while they were searching for a new territory to settle," he finished, sounding disgusted.

"So why hasn't Hart wiped out the village yet?" asked Stanley, a little confused.

"Because there is not enough mass procured yet. Mass takes thousands of years to expand, on its own. It can only be sped up by acts of greed and murder; it will then speed the process up at an alarming rate. Hart believes that his answers lie within the book. He believes that gaining the book will solve his dilemma, and he could finally achieve what he has always strived to for so long. Power. Power over all."

"And will it?" asked Robert, who was watching Desmond interestedly now as well, his eyes wide and eager. "Will it solve his problems and give him absolute power?"

"I do not know for certain," said Desmond, sounding exasperated. "It would most certainly give him an advantage and help him understand the Mass more. What's more, he would be able to make it grow, having all the instruction from the book. If he has been continuing to practice the Forbidden Teachings, which I'm sure he has, he will try to wipe us all out. At least he would rid himself of his resistance. He would enslave the rest of us, for he loves to see people suffer at his doing. He is a very dreadful and vile man."

Stanley stood up quickly and spoke in a brave voice.

"Well, we have to get this Mass back and turn it into the light, so Hart cannot destroy this village."

Desmond, Robert, and Charlie laughed at these foolish words.

"That is something we cannot do," he said gravely, "not with our small numbers. Hart is an extremely cunning and talented individual, not to mention a very smart and experienced shaman. With the Forbidden Teachings at his side, not to mention the alarming amount of men and animals at his side, it would be very hard put to reach him, let alone reach the Mass without sustaining heavy losses."

Stanley was very worried. Desmond could sense the worry in him and smiled at him. When he spoke, it was a calm and comforting voice.

"You need not worry. As long as we keep him and his men confined to their mountain, there is no way Hart can get his hands on this book."

"But if the village goes under attack, wouldn't it be all too easy for him?" Stanley asked, his voice still heavy with worry.

"Hart is not irrational in his planning," Desmond said seriously. "He is clever and cunning, as I have said before. He will drill out every detail in his mind until every little specific is completely flawless. He will not attack unless he is one hundred percent certain of a victory. At this moment in time, however, we are too well guarded. He is too comfortable at the moment. What is more, you carry that book by your side at all times, and only you know its hiding place. There is no way for him to get it."

Stanley could tell by his tone that the conversation was finished. Stanley still felt a little uneasy at this startling news. He did not like the sound of Hart Blackfoot at all, despite never meeting him. He came off as a power hungry and greedy killer, letting nothing stand in his way of total control. There was another loud thud, and a yell of pain from Robert. A second later, Robert stood up, clutching his face and groaning.

"I think it is time for me to head home, my friend," Robert said to Stanley, not looking at him. Upon examining him more, Stanley thought Robert looked strained and confused.

"Are you all right?" he asked him concernedly.

"I'm fine," snapped Robert, sounding unlike himself. Still not looking at him, he said, "Goodnight, Stanley." He turned around and left the hall, Charlie bounding happily behind him, slapping him around as they exited.

"You have any idea what that was all about?" Stanley asked Desmond, who had also watched Robert leave with interest.

"No," said Desmond coolly, "but I would imagine being beat up by a violent kangaroo with deranged tendencies would put a damper on any person's day."

Stanley laughed, though only half-heartedly. Nonetheless, Robert's behavior and sudden change in attitude was startling to

Stanley. Robert had seemed to be having a very intense internal struggle when he had exited the hall. He looked like he was strained to a breaking point.

"I think we should check on him, just to be sure he is all right," he said determinately to Desmond.

"Let him be tonight," said the dog wisely. "Let him calm his own mind. I'm sure he just needs to be alone for a while."

"All right, then," Stanley replied. "But listen, I'm tired of reading. I've had enough for today."

It was true; they had been reading deep into the night and the moon was now twinkling high above the village through the heavily candled window.

"Let's have a drink in the pub," he suggested to Desmond. "I haven't been there recently."

Desmond agreed, and the pair walked through the hall and exited through the massive doors, making their way up the cobbled street. They enjoyed the silence as they walked through the deserted streets. When they reached the pub, they pushed open its heavy wooden doors and entered. The pub was crowded tonight, but they spotted Elliot at his usual seat at the bar, chatting animatedly to Lumen. They looked up as Stanley and Desmond approached, grinning broadly at them.

"All right, brother?" Elliot asked his friend, handing him mead as he sat down.

"Never better," said Stanley, smiling and taking his mead from Elliot.

"Where's Robert?" Lumen inquired, looking around as if expecting Robert to pop up and surprise her.

"He and Charlie headed off to bed," said Stanley in a worried tone. "He is in a funny mood and seems to have a good deal on his mind."

"What on earth could be on his mind?" asked Elliot, sounding amazed. "All he does is get beat up by that animal of his. Poor bloke. Probably thinking of ditching it."

"Can a Speaker do that, then?" Stanley asked his friends at large. "Abandon their companions I mean."

"Aye," said Elliot solemnly. "But it is a very dangerous thing to do."

"Why?" asked Stanley, very interested.

"Because," said Elliot in a very downhearted voice, "when a Speaker abandons their animal, they risk its life. An animal devotes its life to their human, and if it is abandoned, it begins to doubt its own existence, which can lead to the creature's ultimate demise."

Lumen looked shocked; her hand was covering her mouth and her eyes had begun to water. Stanley was distraught, wondering why someone would desert their companion.

"So what happens to the Speaker when he leaves his animal?"

"Nothing at all," said Elliot fiercely. "They are free to find another companion, although if they abandoned one, they are likely to do it again."

"But why, though?" asked Lumen, looking as though she didn't want to know the answer, despite having asked.

"Some Speakers, like our friends in the mountains, use the animals for their own personal gain and then abandon them. Sometimes they will imprison their companions, often treating them cruelly and forcing them to do their bidding under threat of torture. There are some animals, like the lions, that willingly offer their servitude to them in exchange for hunting grounds."

"That's awful," said Lumen, her eyes still watery. She stood up and left the pub, no doubt to find Willow and tell her that she would never leave her.

"That is very nasty," Stanley said to Elliot.

The barman thought Stanley was referring to his mead; he gave him a dark look and muttered darkly under his breath.

"You don't have to drink it you know . . ."

"Yes. It is," said Elliot thoughtfully. "It's very —"

But what it was, they never found out. For at that very moment, a soldier burst through the doors of the pub and darted up to Elliot. He was panting and clutching a stitch at his side, a weasel scuttling in behind him, trying its best not to be trampled as it followed its master.

"There — there — there you are." He wheezed, clutching his side at the stitch now causing him pain, a sword in his other hand. "We've been looking everywhere."

"I've been here all along," said Elliot, looking down at the panting man curiously. "What's going on?"

"We're being attacked," he said in a panicked voice, still panting. "They are coming."

Chapter Ten: Gloomy Tidings

The pub was in an instant uproar. Upon hearing the news, all of the pub's occupants made for the door as one. Benches scraped thickly on the floor, and chairs went flying in all directions as people and animals alike made for the heavy wooden doors, bumping into one another with much clatter and commotion. There was such a clutter about that it took several minutes for Elliot, Oliver, Desmond, and Stanley to get out of the pub and onto the street. They saw no sight of Lumen or Willow. The street was bare, with the exception of the soldier who had warned Elliot of the approaching attack. He was standing near a dirty building that was unoccupied, his weasel running hurriedly around and around his feet, twittering madly. As they made their way to them, they could see the blatant worry and fear on his face. Elliot rushed over to the young man.

"Who is doing this?" he demanded of him strenuously. "Who is attacking us?"

"A tribe of Blackfoot men accompanied by wolves and lions," the young man said solemnly, as if they had already been defeated. "We saw them approaching from the watchtower. They came from all angles. They have surrounded the village. They will break down the gates any minute."

The young soldier was trembling. Stanley saw that the man was only a few years younger than him, in his mid-twenties. He looked terrified knowing that an evil that he only had heard of in stories had now surrounded his home. Elliot pulled out his sword and looked at his friends,

"Well, let's not stand here wasting time staring around. Let's fight them off!" he said in a strong voice that caused inspiration to surge in their blood.

Abruptly, a scream issued from what sounded like the direction of the north gate, immediately followed by the shrill howling from a multitude of wolves.

The young soldier and his weasel began trembling more violently, rooted to the spot, petrified with terror. Elliot grabbed the man by his arm and broke into a run, Oliver gliding above them.

"C'mon then!" he yelled back at Stanley furiously, almost dragging the poor soldier behind him as he bolted through the streets. "We need to find the others!"

They ran as fast as their legs would permit them, winding this way and that through the now crowded and panicked streets. Elliot was in the lead, pushing people and animals from his path as he ran toward the commotion at the gates, which was growing louder as they drew nearer. His sword was gripped tightly in his hands and his cloak was swishing behind him. The terrified young soldier was running behind him, holding his sword in one shaky hand and his weasel in the other. Oliver was above the company, scouting out the battle with his sharp eyes as he beat his wings furiously against the wind now blowing through the village. Stanley and Desmond brought up the rear. Stanley gripped his staff firmly in his hands, ready for the battle.

They expected to be attacked at any minute. Every sharp turn made their hearts skip a beat, hoping beyond hope that the front gate defenses would hold. Desmond's paws were thudding on the ground as he ran and a fierce determination burned in his eyes. The growing sound of screams filled their ears once again, followed by more howling wolves. Stanley's staff was vibrating violently in his hand, as if trying to tell him something. Stanley suddenly realized with a gut wrenching pang that *The Book of Teachings* was exposed in his other hand for the attackers to see.

"The book!" he bellowed at Elliot's retreating back. *"I need to hide the book!"*

They all skidded to a halt. Elliot turned around to look at Stanley. He looked confused and irritated. He had not heard the conversation with Robert and Desmond, after all, and knew nothing about the book's value to Hart.

"What are you going on about?" he inquired of his friend. "Why is hiding the book more important than saving your home and friends?"

"Trust me," Stanley said confidently to him. "Hiding the book may well save this village! I don't have time to explain, but I do know it is what they are after. It is the whole reason they came tonight. It could be the end of us all, if I waltz up to the front gates with it my hands."

"All right then, brother," he said hastily to Stanley. "We are going ahead to help out and do what we can for the others. You hide that book and if you can, keep an eye out for Lumen and Robert. They may not know what has happened yet. But be quick, mate!"

Elliot took a left and darted down a side street, pulling the scared young man and his weasel along and soon disappeared from sight. Stanley and Desmond continued straight for a few blocks and then cut a right onto a side street. They ran past the many people and animals now crowding the streets, all running madly in the direction of the north entrance to help defend the village. They could hear howling and shouts from within the village now. It seemed that the enemy had penetrated the village.

Stanley moved with immense fury toward the Shamans' Hall. He took a sharp left down a narrow street and the magnificent building came into view, its iron gates open wide revealing the heavy wooden doors. As Stanley darted to the gates, a wolf shot out from a side street and ran straight for him. The wolf had his fangs bared, and there was a very nasty red liquid dripping from them: blood. Still running, Stanley sucked the flame from a streetlamp into his staff and shot it at the wolf with the speed and force of a bullet. The flame collided with the animal head on, and it set on fire at once. The wolf howled with agony and terror, as it rolled around madly on the ground, trying desperately to put itself out. Stanley bolted past it and heard Desmond slow down to overtake the beast. He skidded to a halt, turning on the spot to watch his companion.

Desmond looked livid. There was a fire in his eyes as he circled the wolf. He had his fangs bared at it, and his hair was standing on end. He was growling with a fury that he had never revealed before. The wolf attempted to raise itself to its feet, whimpering slightly, his coat now burnt and giving off a very foul smell. Desmond snapped viscously at its legs, and it fell to the ground once more, revealing its belly.

"Leave me!" cried Desmond to Stanley, not removing his eyes from the cowering wolf. "I can manage this filth. Hiding the book is of the utmost importance right now! *Go!*"

Stanley didn't wait around, leaving Desmond to the wolf. He turned round and darted toward the hall's heavy wooden doors. He burst through them with a bang, running like mad toward the door that revealed the spiral stairway to the upper floors. The room was completely barren; it seemed everyone had left to the gates. He knocked into several bookcases as he ran, throwing scrolls and paper into the air and all over the ground. He was longing to go and help his friends; he did not want anything bad to happen to them because of him. All he had to do was hide the book and all would be well. He knew it in his heart.

He slammed the stairwell door open and darted up the spiral staircase three steps at a time. There were no torches lit on the upper levels; it seemed someone had extinguished them. Two floors left — one floor now —

Wham!

As Stanley rounded the steps to his quarters, he was hit with the force of a sledgehammer by some unseen force, knocking him backwards. He toppled down the staircase, his staff slipping from his hand and falling down with a crash onto the floor. Stanley continued to fall down the spiral stairs and as he hit the bottom, *The Book of Teachings* fell from his hand and skidded across the floor. A hand that had recent marks of being bound by chains reached from the shadows and picked it up.

"No!" yelled Stanley as he saw the hand grasp it.

He tried to get on his feet but before he could manage it, he heard a crashing coming down the stairs. He looked up and saw the figure that had knocked him down four flights of stairs directly in front of him. It was Charlie. The marsupial pinned Stanley to the ground with his tail in a heartbeat. He was staring down at him with his fists raised, daring him to move.

Stanley turned his head and focused his attention on the man now making his way slowly out through the shadows and holding *The Book of Teachings* in his hands. Stanley felt his heart drop down to the bottom of his stomach. The man had a very nasty smile on his face and he was staring down at Stanley with rather large, unblinking eyes. It was Robert.

"Hello, Stanley," Robert said in a soft menacing voice, looking at him with humorous interest. "You want to know something,

Stanley? It has taken me a very long time and a great deal of planning, not to mention the most extreme patience, all for a ragged book."

He looked down at the book now in his hands and rotated it, examining it deeply.

"However ..." he continued, looking again at his captive, "my master will be very pleased with me — yes, very pleased."

He gave a smile that did not suit him; it was more alarming than anything. It made him look quite mad.

"Your . . . master?" Stanley spluttered in confusion. "Your master?"

"Yes," said Robert slyly to him, still grinning in that mad and deranged way.

Stanley was still pinned by Charlie and as Stanley looked for a weakness on the animal, he saw that Charlie had several bruises on him and a few nasty cuts. It seemed that Robert had beaten his companion into submission.

"Yes, my master. With good acting and his genius plan behind it all, we now have it: *The Book of Teachings*. The one thing Hart wanted above all else and you lead me right to it." He gave another nasty laugh and kicked Stanley hard in the ribs. Stanley winced with pain.

"But — why did you do this, Robert? Why?" he pleaded to him, groaning slightly from his injuries. He did not understand this. Robert was his friend. He was amazed that such a thing was happening; he had thought Robert was a good person. He had trusted in him completely and thought he was kind and loving. Yet here he was stealing *The Book of Teachings*, all for Hart Blackfoot. This had to be a dream.

Stanley was hoping that he could stall Robert until Desmond was able to come and help.

Robert looked down at him with interest, contemplating something. He then gave a small laugh to himself and addressed Stanley.

"Stanley, Stanley. Do you not see? This was brought on by you and you alone. You, a lesser man, blinded by trust and the urge to see the good in all, have come to show all that your ways will only lead to stupidity and errors. You have failed them all,

Stanley, every person foolish enough to believe that serenity will get you what you seek. Ha!" And he spat in Stanley's face.

"You see!" he bellowed at Stanley with madness. "You have lost, Stanley; you have lost everything."

Just then, Desmond came running through the door, growling as madly as he had been when taking on the wolf. He looked completely unscathed. Desmond bounded onto Charlie and bit him on his leg. Charlie let out a mad howl and kicked Desmond, sending him skidding across the floor. He hopped over to him and lifted him up and tossed him through the large glass window next to the stairway. With a mighty shatter and much howling and whimpering, Desmond was thrown into the street beyond, his body stuck with shards of glass, blood seeping through the wounds. He lay still and did not move.

"*Desmond!*" Stanley yelled with terror, a horrible sinking feeling in his heart. "Desmond, get up! Desmond! Get up, please. Des —"

He was kicked hard again in his ribs by Robert. He looked up at the man now grinning down at him with extreme hatred in his eyes.

"I . . . don't . . . understand," said Stanley quietly, keeled over with immense pain and holding his ribs. "I trusted you, Robert. *I trusted you!*" he bellowed the last words with force at him.

Charlie lifted Stanley up by his cloak, hanging him a few inches above the floor. Robert hit him hard in the stomach, bringing him to his knees, spluttering and gasping for breath. Robert stared directly into Stanley's eyes and smiled nastily once more.

"I lied," he said evilly, still smiling down at him he added, "thanks for everything."

He leaned down and slapped Stanley across the face, hard.

"Goodbye, Stanley."

Stanley felt a very heavy blow to the back of his head, and he was covered in darkness and knew no more.

* * *

"Are you all right, brother?" came a voice from somewhere in the blackness.

Stanley sat up quickly but a hand pushed him back down. He opened his eye and saw Elliot, Oliver, Lumen, and Willow, all sitting calmly on the foot of the stairway and looking very relieved to see him conscious. Desmond was nowhere to be seen. All that remained from the battle earlier was the shards of broken glass from the window. Everything came flooding back to him as he lay there: Robert betraying them to steal the book, Charlie beating Desmond and throwing him from the building.

"Desmond!" Stanley shouted out, making his friends jump. "Have you seen him? Is he okay? Where is he?"

"It's all right, mate," said Elliot calmly to him, still holding him down so he could not get up. "Desmond is fine; he is being healed by the Shaman as we speak."

"It all makes sense," said Stanley in a thoughtful voice, more to himself than to his friends. "All he needed was an animal strong enough to take me down, and his path to the book would be clear."

"Eh?" Elliot said in a rather bewildered voice, "What are you on about?"

"Robert," Stanley replied with a defeated tone. "Robert was a spy; he was working with Hart the whole time. He was the pawn Hart used to steal the book, and he was able to pull it off by gaining our trust."

Elliot removed his hand from his chest and he sat up and sighed. Stanley then told the story of Robert's betrayal. He spoke of how it seemed that Robert had felt no regrets whatsoever at his doings, only the highest honor. He told them of Charlie, being beaten into submission by him, and being bound with a heavy metal collar. He could not believe this; it all seemed like a dream gone horribly, horribly wrong, and they were slowly spiraling down into a nightmare.

"This is a disaster," he said angrily. "It was his plan to befriend me, and I should've caught on. How could I have missed it? This is all my fault," he finished with a feeble voice.

"It's not all your fault, brother," Elliot told him in a somber voice. "We all trusted him, against our better judgment; don't be hasty to take all of the blame."

"Yeah, Stanley," said Lumen, who Stanley noticed was carrying wounds from the battle herself. There was a deep gash on her arm, and her face was scraped and bruised. Willow, as always, was the only one in the company to remain unscathed. "This is the fault of all of us."

They all sat there quietly for a few minutes. They were all thinking the same thing: the next move and the seemingly impossible feat lay ahead of them. Stanley was the one to break the uncomfortable silence.

"We must get that book back to Arda," he said, determined and fierce. He could feel the energy regaining in his body, although he was still stiff in his ribs from his fight with Charlie. "There is really no other choice to make, unless we just let Hart take everything we've grown to care for and love in this place."

"Couldn't agree with you more, brother," said Elliot, smiling at his eagerness to get even with Hart. "We should set off as soon as we are able, but I think it would be wise to help the villagers get themselves back together first."

"Agreed," said Lumen in a confident voice. "We can't do this alone."

"We will ask the town for help, then," said Stanley wisely. "I think they will be just as eager to bring Hart down for good."

"Don't be so sure," replied Elliot darkly. "They may not take too kindly to us once the news leaks about it being our fault."

Stanley thought about these words to himself as they made their way out of the Shamans' Hall. Would the village want to help them now? Or would they frown upon everything? Stanley had a very bad feeling about what was going to come. The damage they beheld as they walked slowly through the streets was heart-stirring. There were fires burning faintly from windows of homes and shops, and glass lay shattered all about the street. People were wandering around, attempting to do all they could to put out the flames. They had crushed, defeated looks about them, and did not acknowledge them as they passed. When the company reached the gate, Stanley's heart sank right into his stomach at the sight he saw.

The front gate had been broken down and set on fire. It was smoldering by the gate's opening. Men were already bringing in planks to rebuild the gate. All around them were people and animals, some sitting on the ground waiting to be healed by the ministrations of the Shaman, holding their wounds. Others lay motionless. There was a soldier lying on the ground a short way away from them, and as they walked past him, they saw with a sickening feeling that it was the young soldier that had warned them of the attack. He lay still and silent on the ground, his weasel next to him. They were dead. They weren't the only ones. There was a man pinned under the wreckage of the smoldering gate, his legs pinned under the wood, a wolfhound by his side. Several soldiers and shamans lay still beside him. The man who ran the apple stand on the main road of the village was wandering around aimlessly, clutching a deep gash on his arm and refusing to let the shaman following him to mend it.

He could be heard repeatedly asking the crowd of injured people and animals, "Where is Nick? Where is my cat?"

There were two shamans sitting against a wall, both sporting bite marks from wolves, and one had a bloody nose and cuts across his face. Lumen's potion teacher, Wilbert Brewst, was next to them. A cauldron was bubbling in front of him, and he was throwing ingredients inside it, stirring with much haste. His small spider monkey was sitting on his shoulder handing him various plants. He spotted Lumen and beckoned her over to him.

"Will you give me a hand with this, dear?" he shouted to her.

"I'll be back soon!" said Lumen hurriedly to her friends as she made her way over to her mentor, Willow trotting quickly behind her.

Stanley, Elliot, and Oliver continued on through the mess and pretty soon, Elliot and Oliver were hailed by guards. He hastily ran over to them, Oliver swaying slightly on his shoulder. Stanley continued to walk around, taking in the destruction. Everywhere he looked there was an animal or person in need of assistance. As he strolled past a turtle that was inching slowly toward his companion who was having a broken arm nursed into a sling by a shaman, he saw a large dog lying alone on a blanket, covered in bandages. It was Desmond.

Desmond looked relieved and happy to see his companion. He gave a feeble sort of wag as Stanley approached him and knelt down. Stanley took out some vials from his shoulder bag and opened them. He then undid Desmond's bandages and poured the liquid onto the dog's wounds. The wounds smoked slightly, and Desmond gave a small whimper. As the wounds smoked, they began to seal themselves, leaving Desmond fully healed. Stanley scratched Desmond's head.

"Good to see you alive," he said to his friend. "I thought for sure you were a goner."

"Thank you," said Desmond, quietly. "I got lucky. If the shaman hadn't come when he did, I would be."

After being assured that Desmond was one hundred percent healed, Stanley left him to heal and began to make his way throughout the crowd of injured animals and people, healing them with his draughts. He passed more of the dead as he healed one after the other. The Animal House Pub owner was kneeling over the man he recognized as the pub's waiter. The small troop of finches was fluttering over them, singing songs of remorse.

After healing multitudes of the villagers, Stanley made his way out of the front gate. About twenty feet from the entrance of the village was a roaring fire nearly fifteen feet high. Soldiers were throwing the bodies of the many wolves, lions, and men that had fallen during the attack. He approached a guard who was talking to Elliot with a rather disgusted look on his face as he stared into the fiery depths at the now smoldering carcasses.

"So they have gone, then?" he heard Elliot saying as he approached the pair of men.

"Aye," grunted the guard rather wearily. "Some bloke riding a kangaroo came through yelling 'It's done! It's done!' They all scattered after that, I can tell you. We chased them as far as the Gloom River, but they already had a fair head start and we soon lost them. There are scouts still out looking for them, but they aren't likely to find much. Those Blackfoots can be terribly sneaky. They can avoid being seen if they wish."

"Not if I can help it," Elliot said courageously, his eyes burning with a fierce determination. "I'm going after them."

"What?" said Stanley hurriedly and confused. "You can't! They will capture you for sure."

Lumen heard the commotion and made her way over to them.

"What's going on?" she asked in a curious voice.

Stanley hastily answered her before Elliot could speak.

"Elliot wants to go after Robert and the Blackfoot men himself, alone!"

"Well that isn't happening," she said calmly. "He's mad if he thinks he's going alone. He wouldn't last an hour without us."

Elliot cut in, somewhat amused, somewhat angry.

"Look, this is all very fun and everything but if we don't get a move on now, we will never catch them."

They all hastily agreed and decided to leave almost immediately. Elliot hastened to tell the guardsmen where he would be and what they would be doing, just in case it turned sour. Lumen ran off to find Willow and to tell Wilbert Brewst where she was heading. Desmond was now walking around with Stanley, fully healed and ready for another adventure. The news of what they were about to attempt had spread like wildfire. Soon enough, the entire village had come to see them off, wishing them luck. Stanley had been wrong; the villagers were not angry at all but alight with hope. They saw them as heroes.

Without any more distractions, the six friends left the village and before they knew it, the cheering had died away, and the village had become nothing more than a pinprick of light in the distance. They were headed up the northern path that eventually led to the desert lands. They would turn left after a few more miles and make their way west, toward the Blackfoot Quarry.

This area was wooded and rocky and was perfect for spending the night. They found a small cave at the base of a forest stream, and they all crammed themselves in. None of them spoke that night as they lay in the dark cave. Their heads were swimming with thoughts of what they were about to do. Was it even possible? Could it be done? Stanley didn't know. He closed his eyes and slipped into uncomfortable dreams. The next morning, they woke up to the worst surprise of all.

Stanley opened his eyes and blinked. Elliot was nowhere to be seen. He had been taken.

Chapter Eleven: Blackfoot Quarry

"*Lumen, get up!*" Stanley shouted as loud as he could, not caring if someone overheard them. "*Lumen! Elliot is gone!*"

Lumen jumped up and rubbed her eyes sleepily.

"Wh—what?" she asked him somewhat groggily. "Who?"

"Elliot!" he bellowed at her. "He's missing. And so is Oliver. We must find them!"

Lumen stood up and they exited the cave, Willow stretching once she came outside. They all blinked in the bright sunlight; there was no sign of Elliot or his belongings.

"What do we do?" Lumen asked Stanley and Desmond who were both scanning the skies for any trace of Oliver. "Where do we start?"

Desmond began sniffing the ground with haste; his eyes narrowed and his ears perked.

"I have his scent," he said suddenly. "Hurry! This way!"

He began trotting through the trees, and they hastily ran to catch up with him. Willow made her way next to him and proceeded to sniff Elliot's trail with him. They followed the two animals slowly as they made their way through the forest. Stanley noticed as they made their way about the trees that the forest seemed to be dying the further they delved into it. The trees had fewer leaves and the forest floor was littered with dead ones, so that the crunching seemed to echo all around them. Suddenly, Willow and Desmond came to a halt with their ears perked, listening intently. Stanley and Lumen crashed into them and fell onto the ground, scattering leaves and dirt everywhere.

"Shh!" said Desmond, and Stanley noticed his voice was anxious. "Quiet! There are people ahead of us."

They hid themselves in a thicket of briar bushes and stared into the distance. Stanley saw that Desmond and Willow had been right. Far off, just before their range of sight failed, they saw three shapes making their way through the forest: two of them human, the other an animal of sorts, but they couldn't make it out fully as it was low to the ground. The first man was wearing a thick black cloak and blood-red robes that bore the paw print marking they had grown familiar with. Most of his face was hidden by a curtain of greasy black hair. He wore long black boots; black gloves sat comfortably upon his hands. There was no sign of a weapon of any kind on him, but they all knew that didn't matter. They knew who this was: Hart Blackfoot. The second man seemed to be cowering slightly at being in his master's presence. When Hart spoke to the man, his voice was pitiless and terrible to behold; there was no trace of kindness or reason in it. It was a dark voice that carried a ferocious power behind it.

"I wonder," Hart said to the man thoughtfully, "if anything that I have ever told you has even penetrated that thick and ignorant skull of yours."

"M—master ..." said the man in a fearful whisper, trembling with fright, cowering almost to the ground. Stanley realized suddenly who the man was: it was Robert!

"M—master, I did it. I stole the book f—for y—you," said Robert, his voice was shaky and terrified. "They will soon be on their way, and all will go as p—planned."

"Yes," came Hart's voice softly, yet a hint of anger was traceable. "You did do this for me, Robert, but you failed me by exposing yourself. They were never to know of your treachery; you were to lead them to me as part of their company, but you did not do this. You resorted to thievery and kidnap, a most primitive way of gaining what you wish. You did not follow my plan. You were foolish. And you will be punished for it. But no matter — I will soon have all I desire."

"Th—they will c—come master," Robert squeaked to Hart. "They will want to rescue their f—friend."

"*Silence!*" spat Hart, and his voice shook with such a rage that the entire forest seemed to cower under him. "You best hope so, Robert, for your sake. Because if they don't, I will be sure to make your life very — unpleasant." He laughed, and his laugh held no happiness but held an evil excitement about it.

"Y—yes m—master," Robert said, trembling from head to foot now.

"Now, get up off the ground and get out of my sight. Keep an eye on our guest," he said nastily to Robert, kicking him as he got up. Robert stumbled but continued to run off in the direction of a massive rocky wall, which no doubt led down into the Blackfoot Quarry.

Hart continued to walk through the trees and a few minutes later, he vanished from sight. Desmond broke the silence.

"We must go back to the cave," he said in a hushed voice to them all. "We should wait for nightfall, and then sneak into the quarry. It will be very dangerous, now that Hart knows we are coming. I'm sure they will have scouts patrolling the outskirts of their borders. Hurry!"

"Thanks for the uplift," said Stanley sarcastically.

They followed Desmond back to the cave, moving much slower this time, their eyes peering through the trees for any sign of a shape that didn't belong. All that day, their thoughts lingered on Elliot. They hoped that he was all right and that he wasn't too close to giving up. That night, when the stars were twinkling brightly in the skies above them, they ate a hurried dinner and proceeded to pack up their belongings once more. They exited the cave and found themselves surrounded by dozens of surly, spear carrying men, all of whom had lions and wolves by their sides. They seemed to have come from nowhere.

"Drop your weapons, you filth! There's no way out," the man closest to them shouted, brandishing his spear at them.

"Well, this isn't good," said Stanley grimly, dropping his staff and throwing his hands up.

Within an instant, the four companions had been chained and bound by the men. The men then made them line up in single file, and then they were blindfolded. All they could hear as they were guided blindly along was the snarling of wolves, the spitting of lions, and the jeering from the evil men.

As they marched along, they bumped into each other occasionally and every time this happened, the men would give harsh laughs and crack whips at their backs, stinging their skin. Soon, they felt the ground growing steadily steeper and steeper. They must have reached the entrance down to the quarry at last. Suddenly, Stanley's foot slipped on loose rocks and he was soon tumbling down a steep slope. As he crashed into something solid and hard, his blindfold was thrown off him, and what he saw when he stood up was a dreadful sight indeed.

High above him, on the peak of the highest rock formation, was a smoky, gassy shape that was letting off small booms that rumbled the ground beneath their feet. Stanley looked at the shape; it was much bigger than Desmond had described it. It seemed as though Hart had already used the book to move the mass to the summit. What was worse, he had expanded it. It would soon be the perfect size to destroy the lands around. Before he could get a better look at it, however, his blindfold was shoved back on his head, and he was struck hard in the back by an unseen force. The blow was incredible; it threw him feet into the air and slammed him rather hard against a rocky wall. He heard the crack of a whip and heard a small whimper from Lumen. He tried to stand up but was pushed down by the sharp point of a spear. There was someone laughing softly near him. He heard a voice speak — a voice he knew all too well.

"Get him up," it said in a soft and amusing whisper. "Let me see him."

Rough hands were forcing Stanley up off the ground now, none too gently, and he was directed a few feet in front of him.

"Well, well, well," said the voice. "Look what we have here, men: a rescue group."

The men jeered and laughed, and Stanley was hit hard in his gut. He crumpled to his knees, clutching his stomach in pain. His blindfold was yanked from his head and he found himself looking up at the sinisterly mad eyes of Robert. He was smiling widely at his captives as he paced around them. As Stanley peered around his surroundings, he saw they were in the heart of the quarry, the center of the Blackfoot village. Charlie was bounding around them, daring any of them to move. He could feel Lumen trembling next to him. He tried to move his hands to comfort her, but they were too tightly bound. The whip cracked again and this time struck Desmond. He gave a terrible yelp of pain and began to whine. Robert made his way over to Stanley.

"It is very nice to see you, Stanley. We have been expecting you," he said nastily to his prisoner.

Stanley didn't say a word. He knew Robert was only goading him to get him angry and besides, he barely had the energy to fight back. He was dreadfully weak and tired from the journey, and the fall down the slopes didn't help anything, either. There was a magnificent *boom*, and Stanley felt the ground quake heavily. Robert looked up at the mass and smiled at it.

"Do you like our little project?" he asked them evilly. "Should be ready any day now." He laughed madly at this. The men and animals around him laughed, too. It was a terrible sound to hear. It was wicked, menacing, and full of hate and anger. Robert turned to the guard who was brandishing the whip.

"Get them out of my sight." He spat.

They were once more forced up onto their feet by the men, and once more they were blindfolded. They were being led into the underground passages and tunnels that led through the mountains and rocks. This was where Hart and his men lived. The tunnels were cold and damp; Stanley could see a dim, faint glimmer of torchlight through his blindfold. They were pushed down steps and thrown around corners as they made their way blindly through the caves. After what felt like forever, they reached a halt. Stanley heard the guard taking Lumen and Willow in cells and slamming the doors, locking a heavy lock with a click. Stanley, too, was thrown roughly into a cell. His hands were unbound and the guard locked the door behind him.

He removed his blindfold and looked around. He was in a very small, rocky cell and he was alone. The door to the cell was a massive wooden one and it was windowless, so he could not hear or see his friends. He sat there with his head in his hands. His belongings had been taken and he was defenseless. This was a complete mess. But then, out of the silence there came a voice that raised his spirits more than anything could at that moment. The voice was scratchy and rough, and sounded strained and weak, but with a heavy trace of happiness in it.

"Stanley?" it said. "Is that you, brother?"

Chapter Twelve: The Return of the Liar

Stanley could not believe his ears — could it be? "Elliot?" he asked the voice to the left of his cell. "Elliot, is that you?"

"Aye," said Elliot and Stanley could tell that he was smiling broadly, despite their current and most unfortunate predicament.

"Elliot!" Lumen's voice came from their right. "Elliot! Oh my goodness, I thought we lost you. Where is Oliver?"

"I'm all right," he said in a strained voice. "I'm a little worse for the wear but all is well. I don't know what happened to Oliver. He must have gotten away."

"How did they get you that night?" Stanley inquired of his friend. "How did they capture you?"

"I don't know. One minute I was sleeping, the next moment, I woke up here in this cell. They have been rather rough with me here. I've gotten three interrogations since I've been here."

"Shut up!" yelled a voice above them. It seemed they were being listened to by the guards above them. The cells must have some sort of vent leading up so that sound could travel. They sat there for hours, still and silent, not daring to make a sound for fear of being tortured.

A little while later, Stanley was fed a small loaf of bread and a canteen of water. He was so hungry that he ate it hastily within seconds. He regretted this decision deeply; as he soon found out they were only fed once a day. He took a gulp of water, settling against the back wall of his cell, thinking hard. As far as he could tell, there was no way out of this accursed place; they had reached a dead end. What was worse, Hart would surely be making his way to Arda within days, with the mass by his side, ready and prepared to unleash its horrible power. He was livid with himself; he could feel the blood boiling in his veins. He stood up and began kicking and slamming his weight into the heavy door, making much noise, and causing rocks and debris to fall on his head from the ceiling of his cell.

"Stanley," came Elliot's voice, sounding very worried, "you must stop making noise, mate. They will hear you, broth—"

But it was too late. In an instant, there was a roar from above, followed by thunderous footfalls making their way toward Stanley's cell. Stanley's door burst open, throwing him backwards against the wall of the cell and causing him to crumple upon the floor. He was then lifted off his feet of his own accord and slammed into the back wall of the cell once more. Once he had caught his breath, it took him a moment to realize that he was completely unable to move. The air around him had formed a barrier of some kind, forcing him upright against the rocky wall of his cell. He focused his mind, trying to break the barrier, but it was no use. Whoever was doing this had skills way beyond his.

A man walked into his cell. He was wearing bright red robes with the paw print of a lion splashed all over them. His hood was down now, revealing greasy black hair and dark, empty eyes. He was smiling at Stanley; his teeth were pointed, like fangs, and the grin he wore upon his face was the wickedest grin Stanley had ever seen any man wear. His left hand was raised, almost lazily, his fingers outstretched, holding his captive in an immobile force of energy.

"Y—you," Stanley gasped, still trying with no result to fight off Hart's hold on him.

"Me," he said nastily, still grinning at him. "Now, if I let you go, you will not escape. If you even try, I will end your life. Is this understood?"

Stanley said nothing, unable to do anything else; he simply glared back at the excuse of a man in front of him.

"*I asked you a question!*" bellowed Hart, and he threw Stanley against another wall with the force of a sledgehammer, letting him slide down it and crumple on the floor once again.

"Y—yes," gasped Stanley, clutching his aching body.

"I have been waiting a very long time to meet you, Stanley," Hart told Stanley thoughtfully, looking down at him with that wicked grin again. "Did you know that?"

"No," said Stanley honestly.

"Well, I have," said Hart. "And may I say you look much like your father — but weaker."

He smiled exuberantly at the look of hatred etched in Stanley's face.

"You know, Stanley, I'm very interested in seeing what will happen when I test the dark mass's capabilities on you."

Hart began laughing manically now, his echoes booming all around the walls. Stanley was thrown back against the wall and onto the hard ground with force and knew no more for quite some time. When he regained consciousness, his cell was locked once more and he was alone again. There was no sign of Hart anywhere.

"Are you all right, brother?" came Elliot's voice from his cell next to Stanley, and he sounded worried.

"I'm fine," Stanley assured him. "Just a little shaken up is all, but I think I'll manage."

A short while later, Stanley was sitting against a wall in his cell, staring around, wondering if he would ever escape from this accursed place. He heard a scuffling of feet outside his cell. A second later, the lock clicked, his cell door creaked open slowly, and someone entered the cell, closing the door behind him. It was Robert.

He was smiling at Stanley but not in that evil way he had when they had arrived; it was kind and warm.

"How are you doing?" he asked in a calm voice. "Are you able to move?"

Stanley jumped to his feet and rushed at Robert, but he was so weak and tired that he could not even make it there; he collapsed onto the ground at Robert's feet. Robert helped him up to his feet.

"What the hell are you doing here?" he asked the nervous man in front of him.

"I'm here to help," he said in an anxious voice. "Please . . . I know I have done much to make you think otherwise . . . I was wrong."

"You think saying you're sorry will make everything you've done better? You think it will bring back those you helped murder?

How dare you!" Stanley spat with fury at him, grabbing him by his tunic and throwing him rather hard into the wall, pinning him there. "I ought to kill you, but that would only make me as bad as you. So instead, you're going to help me escape, and if you cheat us, I will kill you." He let him go and Robert slid to the floor, and then raised himself to his feet once more, staring at Stanley with fear.

"P—please hear me out," he squeaked frightfully as Stanley glared at him. "I know that I have hurt many people and ruined many lives. You must understand; I have been threatened with death from the beginning, ever since I disagreed with his decision to steal the book. He was angry with my impertinence and therefore made me the pawn in his scheme. He made me swear to gain your trust and to lead you here, with the book in hand. But you all showed me I was still a good person inside, and I abandoned the orders. He tortured me when he found out that you were not here and beat Charlie, who has given him all the information he needs about Arda. He knows all their defenses now; he will be ready to destroy them tomorrow. I cannot let that happen. If you trust me, I swear that the mass will never leave this valley — please."

Stanley stood there, wondering about this story.

"Let me out of here," he demanded of Robert. "Now."

Robert took a set of keys from his pocket and unlocked the door, pushing it open, letting Stanley step out. They were in a circular room lined with cells. It was dimly lit; only two torches were set on the wall. Robert began to move around and open the cell doors. Lumen was let out first. She looked bad; her legs bore the unmistakable scars of recent whips, her dress was slightly torn, and there was a nasty bruise under her left eye. Once out of her cell, she rushed at Robert and slapped him hard across his face. He stood, blank faced, staring at her.

"If you ever lie to us again and if we do not get out of here, I will make sure Willow rips you apart. Understand?"

"Y—yes," said Robert solemnly, moving over to Willow's door and letting her out. She was uninjured and looked fairly healthy and happy. She stretched and yawned widely and sat next to Lumen, who hugged her tight.

"Where is Hart?" Stanley asked Robert as he made his way to

Elliot's cell door, put in the key and turned it with a click.

"In his quarters," replied Robert in a strained voice as he pulled the heavy door open.

There was Elliot, sitting on the floor of his cell, looking very worse for wear but smiling broadly at the sight of his friends. He stood up and embraced Stanley in a hug.

"Blimey, it's good to see you, brother," he said heavily. "It is very good to see all of you."

Elliot bore the sign of whip scars on his arms and back. His clothes were ragged and torn, and his trouser leg was torn to reveal the unmistakable sign of being bitten by a wolf. He was limping slightly as he made his way out of the cell. Elliot looked over at Robert, who had stuck out his hand for him to shake, and his eyes flashed with anger. In one swift moment, he punched Robert hard in his face, knocking him to the ground, making his nose bleed profusely. Robert stood up and Elliot moved over to him. Robert cowered but Elliot stuck out his hand kindly, and Robert grasped it. Elliot shook it but did not let go immediately. He grabbed his wrist with his free hand and whispered to Robert.

"If you ever pull that garbage again, brother, I will dismantle you myself, limb by limb."

"Clear," said Robert.

"Cheers," said Elliot merrily now, and he let go of Robert. "Right, mate, how do we get out of here?"

"Follow me," said Robert, darting up the stairway and taking the path to the left, which led down to another circular room with only one cell. The rest of the wall was covered with weapons. Two guards were standing by the doorway. Robert beckoned them to be silent and whispered hastily to them.

"This is the armory where your weapons and Desmond are being held. When I tell you so, come down and retrieve your gear."

Robert darted down the steps three at a time. In an instant, they heard shouting and scuffling, followed by intense barking. Then there was silence.

"You may come down now," he yelled from below.

They ran down the stairway and entered the room; there was Robert, Stanley's staff in his hand, offering his friend to take it. Stanley took it, feeling calmer with it in his hands. He was no longer defenseless. Desmond ran over to Stanley and licked his face, his tail wagging fervently. Desmond looked like he was sore as he moved about; there was a small limp in his step.

"I'm glad you are all right, Desmond," Stanley said to him, hugging his companion in his arms.

"As am I," replied the dog wearily. "I feared the worst, until Robert explained everything to me."

As Robert passed their various belongings around to them, Stanley moved over to him and asked him the question that was on all of their minds.

"What exactly is your plan, Robert?" he asked curiously.

"I'm going to enter the mass and destroy it," he said quietly and determined.

"But that will kill you!" said Stanley. He was shocked and bewildered. "I don't understand."

Elliot and Lumen clearly felt the same way. Elliot was looking at him with confusion, an eyebrow raised in wonder. Lumen stood with her arms crossed, a blank expression on her face.

"There is a way to get rid of the mass before it leaves the mountain," he said hurriedly, trying to explain with haste before anyone discovered them. "Hart has made this mass unstable and because of his arrogance, it could explode at any minute."

"Yes, we know this," said Stanley in an irate voice. "Go on."

"Well," said Robert continuing on quickly, "if I enter the mass with the sole purpose of destroying it, it will explode, shattering me, but my focus will send the energy to one object — your staff Stanley. This is the only way you can stop Hart and finally bring him down."

"What!?" exclaimed Stanley and Lumen together.

"You can't," said Elliot. "We won't let you."

"Look," said Robert hurried and anxious, "this is the *only* way. If you want to succeed, this is the only way to do it."

They stared at him with worry in their eyes; it was inconceivable. Robert was about to sacrifice himself for the better of all of Arda.

"Fine," said Stanley heavily, against his better judgment, "if it is the only way. Lead us on."

"Good," said Robert with determination, turning around and darting up the steps, picking up a sword as they followed him up. "Now it gets real tricky."

"Indeed it does," said a snide and merciless voice from a corridor to their left. A second later, Hart Blackfoot was to be seen, grinning madly, his hands raised at them. The look in his eyes was complete evil. He was going to kill them.

Without hesitation, Stanley acted. Before Hart could react or even move, Stanley shot a burst of energy above him, and a section of the rocky ceiling collapsed upon Hart with an almighty shatter and a great crashing, giving them time to escape. By the time he had freed himself of the weight, his quarry had escaped through the dust and debris.

They ran up the stairs now, Robert in the lead, Stanley and Desmond running next to him. Left, right, up, left, right, up, up, up. Finally they hit level ground. Wind was pouring in from an opening and it was strong; they could barely keep their feet. They were standing on the cliffside Stanley had seen when they came to Blackfoot Quarry. Directly in front of them was the mass, twenty feet tall and wide, swirling and shimmering with a purplish light. Robert yelled to them, above the rushing and booming sounds the mass was producing.

"It is time," he said heavily. "I hope you all will forgive me for everything I've done."

Lumen was crying now.

"Is there any other way?" she pleaded of him, tears running down her face, and her voice shaking. "Surely there must be."

"I'm afraid not, my dear," he said, taking her hand and rubbing her cheek. "I will sorely miss you, Lumen. You are a wonder among normal beings." He turned to face Stanley once more. "When I enter the mass, the process will take place immediately. Light will enter the staff and you will feel its power. Once finished, you will need to get out of here as soon as you can. The mass will explode soon after, so you only have a limited amount of time." He pointed to a passage to his right. "That corridor will lead you down to the bottom of the mountain and back to the main path. From there, you can make your way back to Arda."

He pulled a very tattered book from his tunic; it was *The Book of Teachings*. He handed it to Stanley, who took it and stored it safely in his pack.

"Thank you, Robert," said Stanley sorrowfully. He put his hand on Robert's shoulder. "Goodbye."

"Goodbye," he said sadly and morosely to them all. Then in a determined and final motion, he entered the mass.

The substance swirled around him as he disappeared from view. Then there was a mighty rumble and they heard screaming from inside the mass. A bright golden light emerged from the mass and began siphoning itself into the bamboo staff that was vibrating violently in Stanley's hands. Stanley instantly felt a warming sensation in his body; he could feel all of his wounds healing. He suddenly felt a form of power within him that he could not fully explain. Robert continued to scream for a few more minutes, and then there was only the rushing whirring of the mass. The light ceased and the ground began to quake violently under them. They could feel the mountain begging to crumble beneath them. They lost their footing and fell over. Once they all regained their firm balance, Stanley beckoned them all toward the path that would lead them to their escape.

"Hurry!" he bellowed at his friends. "We need to get out of here. C'mon!"

The five companions darted down the steps of the corridor, running as fast as they all could. As they took a left down another passage, they all skidded to an abrupt halt. They found themselves face to face with Hart Blackfoot. He grinned at all of them in a menacing way, revealing those pointed teeth.

"Well, well, well," he spat with pleasure at the fear in their faces. "This is about to get very . . . unpleasant."

The corridor echoed with his mad laughter.

Chapter Thirteen: The One in Charge

Hart gave a small whistle and from the shadows emerged the largest lizard Stanley had ever laid eyes on. It was as big as Willow and its body was heavily armored in thick heavy scales. It hissed violently at them as it waddled over to its master with an incredible speed. Hart smiled with delight and stroked the lizard's head.

"This," he said, gesturing to his animal, "is Comet. He comes from the desert lands. I found him when lost there, witless and wandering. He is a Star Dragon, the rarest of all lizards. And he will rip you apart for your foolishness." He laughed evilly and hissed darkly to his beast, "Rip them apart."

The battle began at once. The lizard jumped at Stanley swiftly, but Elliot came rushing from the side and collided with it. It hissed violently and began snapping madly at his feet. Elliot swished his sword, but the lizard darted away with the speed of a bullet and made its way toward Elliot. Willow moved with a mighty roar toward the beast. In one heavy movement, she brought her paw through the air and it collided with the lizard, throwing it aside. She rushed over and pinned it to the ground. It writhed madly, trying to break free. Desmond bolted over and began tearing at the lizard with his teeth. It howled with agony for a few moments, and then it moved no more. There was a madding roar, and Hart advanced on Stanley.

Stanley shot a burst of bright light from his staff at Hart. It hit him hard in the face and he fell backwards, clutching his face where a shiny burn had appeared. Before Stanley knew it, he was beating Hart with his staff. Every time the staff made contact with him, there was a blinding flash of light, followed by a shriek of pain.

Hart's lizard broke free of Willow's grasp, having bitten her in her leg. She gave a furious howl, lifted the lizard from the ground, and tossed it with intense strength at the wall. It collided hard and slid down to the ground. Elliot darted over and swished his sword. The lizard was split in half at the waist and moved no more.

Lumen rushed over to Stanley who was continuing to beat Hart lifeless. Lumen removed the staff from his hands. Stanley started, staring at Lumen with wonder. Hart lay on the ground twitching and groaning. He had been weakened by the immense power of the light. It seemed to drain all of his power from him.

"What are you doing?" he asked her, irritated and angry. "Give me my staff back."

"No," she said firmly. "You can't kill him, Stanley. It would make you just like him."

"*I don't care!*" he bellowed at her. "I'm going to kill him; he deserves it. He's done too many awful things to be spared."

"No one is denying that, brother," said Elliot, walking over to him and wiping the blood of the lizard from his sword. "But Lumen is right. We can't kill him."

"Every life is worth saving," said Desmond.

There was a rushing noise, followed by a whimper. They were knocked backwards without warning. When they stood up, they saw Desmond lying unconscious on the hard stone floor, a rock lying by his head. Hart was standing now, clutching the burns on his arms and face. Stanley gave a yell of fury and shot a beam of light at the man; it hit him square in the chest. Hart was lifted from the ground majestically and slammed down into the ground, where he lay motionless, but alive.

There was the sound of a sword being drawn and a second later, they looked around to see Elliot holding the tip of his sword at Hart's throat.

"You move — you die," he said in a menacing voice, digging the tip of the sword into his neck slightly, so that small drops of blood were seeping down his neck.

Stanley walked over to his pack and withdrew some rope. He then bound Hart's arms and feet. They lifted him to his feet and he stared around at them, still smiling evilly. The ground trembled violently and the whole mountain shook. Stanley looked around at the others.

"We must get out of here," he said quickly.

He lifted his staff and struck Hart on the head. Blinding light flashed around them and revealed Hart out cold. They tied him to the back of Willow.

"If he comes to, kill him," Stanley told the bear.

And without any more hesitation, the five friends made their way through the passageways, darting this way and that. Hart was bouncing on Willow's back, his head lolling from side to side, occasionally hitting it on a wall as they rounded a sharp corner. Stanley looked down at Desmond who was running with haste next to him.

"Can you get us out of here?" he asked.

"Yes," said Desmond simply and taking the lead, he stuck his nose into the air and sniffed.

He began to lead them on, turning this way and that way. The mountain was vibrating violently now, and several rocks began falling on their heads. They turned a sharp corner and saw a terrible sight. There was a mound of rocks covering the lower body of an animal. It was Charlie. He stared at them with his round eyes.

"Get out of here — leave me," he pleaded.

They continued to run, leaving Charlie to die in peace. They bolted down a free corridor on the right and found the passage widening. They had reached the bottom of the mountain. They could see an opening a few feet ahead and they bolted toward it with all the speed they could muster. But as they reached the opening, they saw a sight that made them stop in their tracks. All of Hart's men were waiting for them, swords and spears raised. All around them were wolves and lions, spitting madly and howling with evil glee. The battle wasn't over yet.

Chapter Fourteen: The Battle of Blackfoot

The corridor rumbled with anger and the mountain began to crumble and shatter above them.

"Well, it's now or never," said Stanley confidently.

Without another word, they made their way out of the cave into the battle. They began fighting at once. Elliot was clashing swords with four men, kicking the lions advancing on him as he fought. Stanley was firing his staff at anything he could. Flash after flash, men and animals dropped. Lumen was firing her bow at the speed of light, sinking one arrow after the other into her enemies. Willow was in the lead, bowling people over with immense power, Hart still tied to her back. Even though the company fought with extreme effort, they were heavily outnumbered. Sooner or later, they would have to surrender to the men. An arrow zoomed by Stanley's head as the mountain gave one last violent shudder and began to collapse.

The men began to scatter in all directions, making their way to the path leading to Arda. Stanley bolted after them, his friends moving swiftly behind him. They made their way through the paths, taking out as many of Hart's associates as they could. The Blackfoot men had soon disappeared from view, having known all the secret passages in their land, making it simple for them to escape. Pretty soon Stanley and his friends were all alone again. There was a screech from above and they looked up. Oliver was soaring down to Elliot. He landed with grace onto his master's arm. Elliot stroked the bird's plumage happily.

"It's about time you showed up," said Elliot exuberantly. "I've been having all the fun to myself."

They continued on up and up, to the large opening that led to the valley and toward Arda.

When they reached the opening, they looked back at the ruined mountain. All that was left was a large mass of rubble. With a dreadful pang, Stanley thought of Robert and what he had given up to keep them safe. A tear ran down from his eye and he wiped it off, looking in the distance toward Arda. It warmed him to know they were making the return journey home.

That night went fairly smoothly. They set up a camp a few miles from the village and tied Hart to a tree. He remained unconscious throughout the night. They would take him to Arda for trial. There he would be sentenced. They went to sleep that night completely comforted.

The next thing he knew, Stanley was being shaken awake by Elliot.

"Get up, mate; we got trouble," he said in a worried tone.

Stanley stood up and gasped at what he saw. The entire Blackfoot settlement had surrounded them as they slept. They stood there, transfixed at their new predicament.

"Reckon we have one more good fight in us?" Elliot said to his friends, smiling at them broadly.

They all smiled at one another and raised their weapons, prepared for the fight. Lions, wolves, and men were closing in, teeth bared and weapons raised. Stanley didn't know how they would make it out of this alive. It seemed that this would be their final fight.

They fought with all of their might, but their strength was waning. Soon they would be overtaken; there were too many of them advancing. Swords clashed and arrows zoomed; all the while they fought on. When they felt as if they could not lift their weapons anymore, they heard a sound that made their hearts leap.

There were voices coming from the top of the hill growing louder and louder as they drew near, behind the attackers. They were not evil voices, however; they were battle cries. With a leap that rejuvenated his body, he saw that it was the entire village of Arda making their way down the hill. Every occupant of the village was running with haste down to the battle. Speakers and their animals, non-Speakers carrying weapons, all yelling with fury, determined to flush out the enemy from their beloved land and save their friends. The Blackfoot men turned around with haste and reformed their ranks, preparing to take on their new offense.

Stanley and his friends began fighting once more with renewed vigor, taking anyone down in their way. Stanley saw the owner of The Animal House Pub, Arland Whistleworthy, and his chimp by his side, both wielding swords and taking on two wolves and men. Several shamans were blasting fire toward a group of lions that howled with pain and agony as their coats set on fire. Wilbert Brewst and his spider monkey were in a furious tussle with several men, rolling on the ground, their fists flailing madly. A large group of non-Speakers were wielding swords and clashing spears with men and lions. Elliot had begun directing the soldiers who had made their way down to him. Oliver was soaring above him, zooming down upon his enemies, tearing at them with his talons and beak, sending them running off shrieking and yelling. The front gate guard was taking on a group of wolves with his hippo. The owner of the unmanageable animal tent was chasing after his moose as it bowled though the evil men, sending them flying in all directions.

The battle began working in their favor and soon enough, the Blackfoot men were surrounded. Without a word, they ran for it, back toward the direction of the Quarry. The villagers chased after them, shooting magic toward their retreating backs and yelling with mirth, leaving Stanley and his friends with the guardsmen and non-Speakers that remained behind.

Stanley and Desmond began to help the villagers who had been left behind, too wounded to chase after their attackers. The battle went on heavily into the night, much of it in Arda's favor. Finally, the Blackfoot men retreated with haste, leaving many of their dead and wounded behind. Hart was being guarded by Willow, still tied mercifully to the tree. The Blackfoot men and animals that remained were captured and bound and placed in a group by the tree where Hart sat, still unconscious from the blow received from Stanley's staff.

Once the village had gathered itself again, they all proceeded to make their way back to Arda. Stanley, Desmond, Oliver, Elliot, Lumen, and Willow led the way, dragging the unconscious Hart behind them. Finally after a few hours, when the sun had begun to rise, they reached the gates of Arda. The villagers began to clap and cheer as they made their way through the streets. They smiled broadly as they made their way through the village, waving and hugging their supporters and healing the wounded. They were hugged and thanked by every occupant of Arda, Speaker and non-Speaker alike.

"Told you they would come around," said Elliot, grinning broadly at his friends.

Stanley looked around at the villagers; all of them bore signs of battle. He felt a fond rush of love for them all. They had all fought alongside him for the same cause. He was holding *The Book of Teachings* in his hands. He looked down at his dog, who was wagging his tail happily at the attention he was receiving. Stanley knelt down and hugged Desmond.

"We are home," he said to him happily, as Desmond licked his face.

* * *

Stanley and Desmond were sitting in their quarters a few days later, basking in the warm sun that was flowing in through the open window. The warm rays relaxed their bodies and calmed their minds. They heard someone heading up the spiral stairway and a moment later, there was a sharp knock on his door. Desmond barked.

"Who is it?" Stanley inquired at the door.

"Elliot, brother," replied his friend's merry voice. "May I come in?"

"Of course," said Stanley, getting to his feet and crossing over to the door and opening it, letting Elliot inside.

Elliot was smiling broadly at him.

"Want to go for a walk?" he asked his friend.

"Sure," said Stanley and turning to Desmond, he said, "Wanna go out for a walk?"

Desmond bounded off the bed he had been lying on, his tail wagging madly and his eyes burning with excitement.

"That is the stupidest question to ask a dog, you know," he said smartly to Stanley, and he bounded down the staircase. Elliot and Stanley pursued him.

Once outside, they made their way toward the south gate, where they had first set eyes on Arda. The villagers outside waved merrily to them, smiling happily. They returned their smiles as they walked and before they knew it, they had reached the gate. They spotted Lumen and Willow a short way ahead, propped against a tree outside of the gate, their eyes closed, enjoying the sun's rays.

"Where's Oliver?" Stanley asked Elliot in wonder, looking at the sky for a sign of the falcon.

"On duty," replied Elliot, "scouting, you know."

Elliot, Stanley, and Desmond made their way over to Lumen and Willow. Elliot sat down and lit his pipe, taking a long pull on it before sighing deeply to himself. Stanley pulled out his own pipe and lit it, blowing smoke rings into the air. Elliot sighed in a relieved way, pulled on his pipe again, and addressed his friends.

"Hart's trial will be in a few months," he said as he exhaled smoke from his nostrils. "Until that happens, what is next?"

"Well," said Stanley thoughtfully, "I would like to visit Oakhill in the near future."

His mind had often wandered to Lila and Prentice in the past few days, and he was anxious to see them and tell them of his travels and adventures.

"We should visit the Silver City after that," said Desmond.

"What's in the Silver City?" Stanley inquired, but it was Elliot who answered.

"Ports for ships — ships that lead to Elda," he said, knowingly.

They decided that this would be their next road. Once they visited Oakhill, the travelers would make their way through the Nowhere Lands, which were covered with thick desert. Once through the desert, they would go to the Silver City; from there the road would lead them to Elda: the original land of the Speakers.

Just then, Oliver returned from his scouting. He soared down and perched himself on Elliot's shoulder. They all sat quietly against the tree and watched the sun setting on the western horizon.

When the sun had disappeared from view, the company remained sitting and laughing. After a few hours, they made their way in to the village for a drink in the Animal House Pub. The six friends sat at a small round table, drinking and laughing together deep into the night.

The last thing that was to be done was mourning. The next

day, there was a large ceremony outside the village in the amphitheater for those who had been lost in the battle of Blackfoot. The village gathered together to mourn the loss of their friends: Speakers, non-Speakers, and animals of all sorts. Stanley, Desmond, Lumen, and Willow sat in the front row. Elliot was to give the opening speech to the village.

"Good evening," said Elliot to them all in a caring voice that was full of remorse, but steady. "We are here today to remember those who fought gallantly for our beautiful land. We are here to remember the animals, the men, the women, the shamans and the soldiers, the Speakers and the non-Speakers. All of these people believed that the evil of the world will never prevail against the persistence of those who wish for love and peace — those who always had love in their hearts. We shall remember those lost and drink to their spirits forevermore. Never forget their courage and bravery. Know that they did not die in vain, but that they died for peace and love. We thank their efforts and will always remember what they gave up."

He stepped down off the stage as the village clapped quietly and took a seat next to Stanley and Lumen. As the next man took to the stage to speak, Stanley looked down at Desmond, his eyes watering and his heart rushing with warmth.

"Desmond?" Stanley said to his dog.

Desmond looked up at him, his tail wagging slightly.

"Yes?" he asked his companion.

"Thank you for choosing me," he said to him, reaching down and scratching his dog behind his ears. Desmond licked Stanley's hand.

As Stanley looked off into the distance toward the lands he had left so long ago, he smiled to himself. All was how it should be, as the birds soared above them, singing their songs of remorse. Everything was well. Hart was captured and in prison, *The Book of Teachings* and the village of Arda were safe. He was with his friends, but most importantly — above all other things — he was with his dog.